CHARLIE the HORSE, OWL and the PLANNING APPLICATION

a fable for our times

story by

Lindsay Dowding

and illustrations by

Lynn Rutherford

Cover illustration by G E W Lain, SGFA, also known as "The Hairy Upright".

Smokehouse Press
Norwich

Published by Smokehouse Press, Norwich, 2019

www.smokehousepress.co.uk

Typeset in Times New Roman by Smokehouse Press

Printed and bound in England by CMP (uk) Ltd

ISBN 978-0-9576335-8-2

Previous titles from Lindsay Dowding,
Talking to Emelda

and from Lindsay Dowding, Lynn Rutherford and Jo Aldred,
Three Women on the Cusp

Lindsay Dowding and Lynn Rutherford having fun and talking about Charlie, Owl and their friends.

Thanks and acknowledgements

As the writer in the team who have created this book, I felt that it should be me who writes this small tribute to the people who have made it possible.

My especial thanks go to my dear friend Lynn for all the enthusiasm she maintains for a new project however odd it seems at first sight. I am enormously grateful to Graham and Betty Lain for their hospitality and good humour. Graham's paintings are always a delight. Also of course my thanks go to Robbie the dog.

The BBs Craft Group has been endlessly entertaining, witty and wise and has listened to Charlie the Horse as the writing and illustrating progressed. Our publisher and friend, Thea Abbott has been patient and encouraging.

And of course none of this would have been possible without my husband John who ferries me about and happily gives help and support.

And last, but by no means least, my thanks go to The Norfolk and Norwich Hospital Stroke Unit for helping Lynn, me and all the stroke patients who have benefited from their excellent care. As a token of thanks I have decided that half the first year's proceeds will be donated to help them with their work.

Lindsay Dowding
February 2019

Charlie's 'family', Darren, Charlie, Mel, Sophie and Luke.

INDEX

1	Welcome	1
2	The poster	7
3	Idea number one	13
4	Idea number two	21
5	Owl gets cross (but not for long)	37
6	Owl's great dilemma	45
7	Bats	53
8	Making plans	71
9	A prickly problem for Slippers	75
10	Mrs Owl gets cross (for quite a long time)	87
11	Slippers goes wooing	93
12	Owl's idea	101
13	Action begins	109
14	Hen has a plan	117
15	The day of the Theodolite	123
16	What's next?	137
17	Fred visits the boss	141
18	The Environmental Yellow Hat	151
19	A site of Special Scientific Interest!	157

A SKETCH-MAP OF WHERE IT ALL HAPPENS.

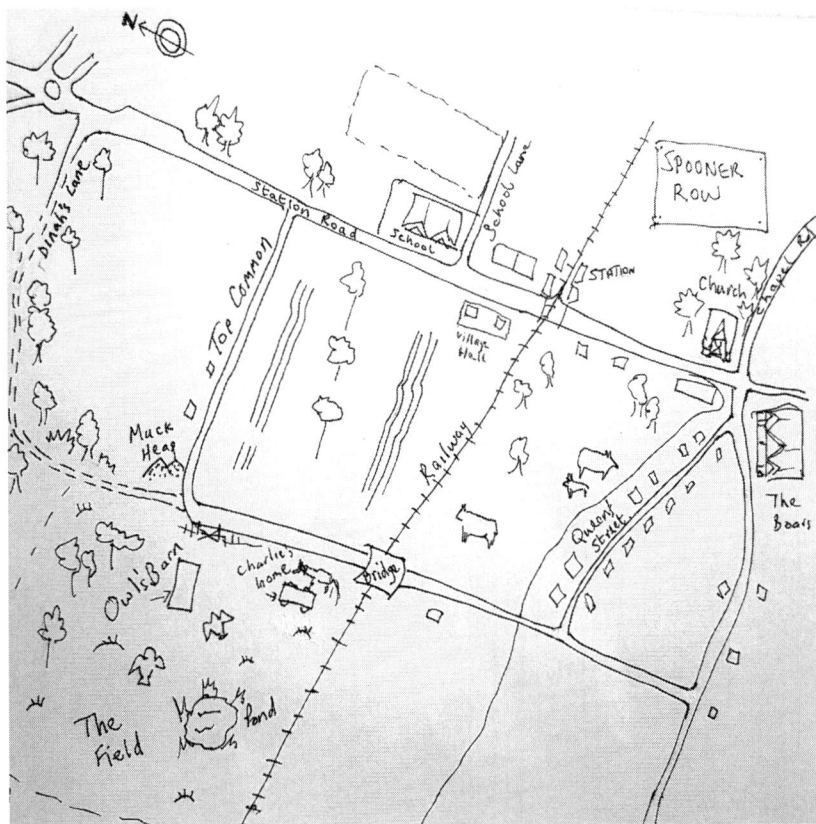

1. WELCOME

Charlie enjoyed his life. He had a two-acre field to himself with his own detached home in a roomy, rusting horse lorry, minus its wheels. His water supply was a large bowser on a wheeled trolley and this was kept topped up by his owner, Mel who worked very hard at the local hospital but still found time to visit Charlie to groom him and chat to him. Sometimes he thought she looked tired but usually, by the time she left she looked cheerful again. Mel's mate was called Darren and he worked at the hospital as well and they had two of the small Uprights, a soft one called Sophie and a hard one called Luke. They weren't on wheels any more and didn't seem to scream and shout as much as the very small ones – much to Charlie's relief. He felt very lucky to have this little family of Uprights to look after him. They couldn't always get over to see him, but if they couldn't then other Uprights like Tallulah or even the Hairy Upright with Robbie came instead and he guessed they must have arranged this.

 He liked Tallulah because she was pretty, talked to him as she groomed and stroked him, and though he couldn't always understand everything she was saying he sort of got the gist of it. Sometimes she had mints, which they shared. Mel brought carrots or apples and Charlie sensed that they were somehow better for him – but not such fun!

He had no other equine companion, which was a shame but he thought that he might lose some of his privileges if he had to share his home. Mel had once provided him with a donkey called Cyril as a companion but as Charlie had suspected he proved to be a poor substitute for a horse, a creature of low intellect, given to making the most terrible braying and honking noises when amused or excited, for example when Tallulah came with her pockets bulging with treats. Cyril's conversation was minimal and his accent so strong that Charlie struggled to understand him.

It was quite a relief when Darren came with a small horsebox towed behind the battered jeep and loaded Cyril on board. He had watched as Cyril was trundled off down the lane, his head joggling as the wheels went over ruts and pot-holes. He never returned.

Charlie wished him no harm and hoped that perhaps he had been taken in by a family of mixed Uprights such as he saw quite regularly in the lane. There were usually two tall ones – one soft and one hard and several small Uprights who often needed wheeled scooters or even prams to get about. He wasn't so keen on the small Uprights – they screamed and cried a lot and made noises which reminded him of Cyril.

There were always the Hens of course. They lived in a special wired off enclosure inside the field and generally came under the wire two or three times a week to peck around in the mud churned up by Charlie's hooves. There was Hen who had glossy brown feathers, Black Hen, larger, sleek and shiny black and Slippers a little speckledy Bantam with ruffles of feathers round her feet. Hen sometimes strutted her way up the ramp into his trailer to peck amongst the straw. He resented this and once tried to discuss the intrusion with Hen but, much like Cyril, the conversation was limited and the accent unfamiliar so he had given up trying to discuss the matter. In any case he quite enjoyed the occasional visits as a diversion. Once to his horror Hen had completely forgotten herself and had laid an egg right beside his trailer door. Most embarrassing! It had lain there in some wisps of straw for several days and he had eyed it with disapproval and some anxiety. Charlie had a vague idea that there was a new hen inside the egg who had to get out at some stage. He strongly doubted this given the size and shape of the egg. It would have to be a tiny hen but it didn't move or show any signs of life and then one morning it had gone! Vanished, no trace, disappeared.

Perhaps the small hen had got out of the egg and taken the rest with it. Anyhow he forgot about it in a few days but the next time Hen came he had a stern word about indiscriminate egg laying and the importance of good manners and restraint. There had been no repeat of the episode.

Charlie had one companion whom he considered to be his intellectual equal (if not indeed his superior though he tried not to think about that) and this was Owl. Now Owl had quite a desirable, detached stone built residence in the next field and this was an old abandoned barn. Some official looking Uprights in green uniforms had come one day and, so Owl had told him, had fixed up a special wooden box in the eaves in a corner of the barn. It even had a special number stamped on the front by the door – E1693340. Charlie quite envied the number. He hadn't seen it of course but Owl had told him about it.

"Hard to remember," Charlie had said. Owl agreed but said he had thought of a good 'mnemonic ' to help him. Charlie liked to think that he and owl had a similar intellect and didn't ask the meaning of 'mnemonic' so as not to appear dim.

"The number is useful if any of my friends or family send letters," said Owl.

Now Charlie had never received a letter in all his time at the trailer and felt quite put out (also he wasn't quite sure what a letter was). He compromised by nodding sagely and saying, "Yes indeed, most useful."

Charlie bent down and tore off a juicy clump of grass and when he looked up Owl had vanished. Not even a whisper of sound. Animals had quite a strict code of conduct amongst themselves (birds too) and so he made no comment, merely looked up towards the small, plain church at the crossroads and spotted the smooth, wide wingspan gliding overhead and dipping down behind The Boars.

Owl visited Charlie daily at about 5.30 in the morning. Charlie would stretch and peer about in his trailer and then lumber down the ramp to sniff at the morning air and Owl would be perched on the top bar of the post and rail fence, preening his feathers a little to be ready for the day. In the summer he was clear and fluffed out as he preened and in the winter he was a soft silvery glow in the darkness. They didn't chat much at that early hour saving that for later when after about three quarters of an hour Owl would suddenly glide down on to the fence rail and fix his sharp, wise eyes on the horse, waiting to see who would speak first.

2.   THE POSTER

One morning in early April Charlie felt that Owl was a little late returning from his morning flight. Of course he had no clock to look at and the little church had long since stopped chiming the hours but animals sense time quite accurately and he looked up occasionally at the fence and above it to the dark fields beyond. There was a low mist that had crept across the countryside, gradually dispersing as it came and Owl suddenly appeared and settled on the top rail looking slightly ruffled. Charlie allowed time for him to settle (which was only polite).

"Alright Owl?" asked Charlie kindly.

Owl clacked his beak, let out a very quiet screech and changed feet several times on his perch.

"Not sure Charlie," he replied.

This was alarming; firstly Owl never screeched unless for a good reason and secondly Owl was always sure. If he wasn't sure then this might rattle the whole of their day's placid routine.

"Take your time old friend," said Charlie and noticed that Hen had made an unusually early appearance, scratching her way across to the trailer pecking the earth but looking jerkily up at Owl in between pecks.

Owl had settled himself now, his feathers were smooth and he turned the flat disc of his face towards the two companions.

"I saw something white fluttering on a post over there as I came in to land. I remembered an Upright banging away at the same post yesterday. You know what a noise they always have to make," the others nodded, "Anyhow, I went over and perched and had a look,"

A long silence followed and at last Charlie said, "Well Owl, what of it, what was it?"

Even Hen said, " Yes, what?" This was one word more that she usually said.

Taking a deep breath Owl replied, "I'm not quite sure because it kept blowing about, not properly fixed you see, shoddy Upright workmanship! But," he said heavily, "It was headed: PLANNING APPLICATION!"

They looked at Owl blankly, "And it mentioned this and adjoining fields, totalling 5 acres. The question is, which way is it adjoining – which just means 'joining to' you know," he added kindly.

Charlie and Hen both looked rather huffy as if to say, "We know, we know."

"As I was saying, does it 'adjoin' those fields down by the muck heap, where Wycke Hall used to stand OR does it mean this way, where we live, where our homes are, OUR fields!"

Owl let out another slightly louder screech and fixed them with a fierce stare. Hen had only understood a very small part of this speech but had caught 'Our homes, our fields' and saw that Owl and Charlie looked upset and worried.

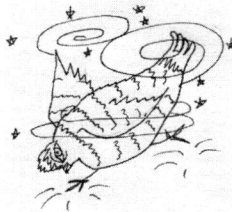

Her response was to flap her wings wildly, making little runs and jumps, pecking frantically at the ground. She ran round and round for a minute and then clucking loudly squeezed under a loose bottom rail of the fence and disappeared. Owl and Charlie allowed a minute or two to elapse as was only polite, and then making no comment about Hen resumed their conversation.

"What do you understand Owl by 'PLANNING APPLICATION?"

It showed his level of anxiety that he allowed Owl to realise that his knowledge of planning matters wasn't all it was cracked up to be.

Owl puffed out his chest feathers and continued, "I believe that a number of the older looking Uprights get together in a building and decide if they agree with the request and if they do then all those building Uprights, the ones in the yellow hats, appear with lots of machines and build rows and rows of houses. Then," he added importantly, "Other Uprights who usually have a lot of those smaller, shrieking ones on wheels come and live in them."

"But," said Charlie, "There would be no grass, no barn. What would we do? Where would we go? Would they put us in places far apart? We might never meet again!"

Now, as we all know, animals tend to avoid emotional displays but Charlie and Owl had been companions for several years and had enjoyed their quiet friendship.

"What about Hen?" said Charlie.

"Well sometimes Uprights make little houses for hens, I've seen them as I fly over but she couldn't go off visiting she'd have to stay put and it would be much smaller than she's used to."

Charlie sighed and blew air down his nostrils, shaking his head and stamping the ground he turned and plodded back up the ramp to his straw bed in the trailer. He needed to think.

Likewise Owl rose up in to the air and soared over to the barn and the peace and quiet of E1693340 to doze and ponder and ponder and doze until the evening fell over the fields again.

Charlie, thinking about things outside Owl's barn.

3. IDEA NUMBER ONE

After a restless night of tossing and turning on his straw bed in the trailer, Charlie finally surrendered and decided he might as well get up. He had woken suddenly from a doze with a terrible start and immediately thoughts such as, "What will happen to our home? Where shall we go?" had begun circling wildly in his mind.

He plodded wearily down the ramp and looked around in the early morning light, it was still very misty. He could make out Owl's shape on the fence and was it his imagination, or did his sleek form look a little slumped this morning, most unlike Owl. He refrained from commenting.

"Morning Charlie," said Owl.

"Morning Owl," said Charlie.

He stretched his head up to the sky, shook his mane and blew down his nostrils, then set off for a light trot around the perimeter of his property.

Owl screeched softly and edged back and forth on the fence. He fluffed his feathers and straightened up.

"Had an idea in the night, while I was flying about you know."

"Oh yes?" said Charlie, pulling at a tuft of grass and chewing absently.

"I decided that I'd pull down the planning poster and keep an eye out to see if they replace it. If they do, I'll have it down in a wink. That'll show 'em!"

"Good thinking Owl. They have to put up a poster for Uprights to know their plan so if you keep tearing it down they might give up altogether."

"Right!" said Owl, "I'll go and get it now."

And with that he took off soundlessly into the air and glided down towards the muck heap. He returned in no time with the white poster flapping in his beak. It was a bit tattered at the top.

Owl flew down on to a bale of hay next to the trailer and dropped the poster at his feet. Standing on the top edge with his claws digging in to the paper he called to Charlie, "Hi, come and look at this thing!"

Charlie was already walking over and peered at the poster.

"Hm," he said and then "Hm," again.

He couldn't understand all the very formal wording but got the gist of it sufficiently to feel the alarm rising in him.

"Looks very official," he said.

"Well naturally," said Owl. "You know these Uprights always like to make a song and dance about everything but basically their intention is plain to see isn't it?"

"Certainly is," said Charlie gloomily.

"Well," said Owl, "It's a start!"

"Oh yes indeed," said Charlie, not wishing to sound unenthusiastic but secretly thinking that seeing it in writing made it all the more frightening, and wondering if this strategy would be enough.

"Robbie's coming with the Hairy Upright," called Owl who could see over the hedgerow and along the lane from his vantage point on the bale. He took off quickly and landed back on the top fence rail as usual.

Charlie mosied around by the trailer and looked up as the Hairy Upright leant his arms on the fence and nodded peacefully at them.

They all liked Robbie the dog and the Hairy Upright. Robbie, like most dogs (with a few notable exceptions) was intelligent and quietly sociable. He brought his Upright out twice a day for exercise and didn't bark unnecessarily or try to fight with every other dog he met. They were quite an unusual pair. They walked briskly along together, clearly in tune with each other and enjoying the countryside around them.

Mostly, the animals had observed, that dogs had to drag their Uprights out on walks. You could almost hear them coming, panting and straining at their reluctant charges, having to pull them along to keep them going. They had to stop quite often to let the poor things rest and filled in this time by sniffing and peering around in the dykes surrounding the fields. When the Uprights were ready they started off again but the dogs still seemed to have to chivvy them along, running back and forth constantly. It all looked like terrible hard work and they had often discussed this odd practice.

Did the dogs enjoy this responsiblility? Where did they get the Uprights from? They supposed that it was beneficial to the dogs who presumably got fed and housed free of charge but personally they preferred their more independent life.

It was fun to watch if a tractor or a car came along. The Upright would panic like mad, calling to the dog and dragging at it to come and protect it. The dogs went along with it, and generally the Upright was soothed and they carried on their way. Sometimes one of the dogs would look back at them over its shoulder and roll its eyes as if to say, "Aren't they ridiculous, but I'm fond of him or her, and what would they do without me!"

Sometimes, if Mel couldn't come for a few days, the Hairy Upright and Robbie would appear instead. They would put down hay and feed for Charlie and sorted out Hen, Black Hen and Slippers, collecting any eggs and tidying up generally. The Hairy Upright would chat to Charlie companionably and while he saw to the hens, Robbie would stop for a bit of a chinwag. Owl and Charlie could understand Robbie quite well, but, like all dogs they met, his speech was a curious mix of animal and human and this made it a little harder to follow.

This morning, the Hairy Upright didn't speak, he just leant on the fence quietly and then Robbie took him away to continue their walk. The Hairy Upright was a perceptive fellow though, and had noticed the poster on the hay bale and had also seen the tattered remnants still attached to the nail in the telegraph pole by the muck heap.

There seemed little else to say or do after this first bit of excitement so Owl went back to E1693340 and settled cosily down to sleep. He was a little comforted by the thought that some sort of campaign had begun. They would think again tomorrow.

4. IDEA NUMBER TWO

The next morning, Owl had decided to go straight home after the night's foraging and have a sleep, then get up in the afternoon and visit Charlie. He disliked changing his routine, it put him on edge but he wanted to see if Black Hen was about and could come up with any further ideas. No good asking Hen – she was not the brightest of birds and tended to get a bit hysterical if worried, but Black Hen was another kettle of fish; (what was a kettle of fish and why were they in there?). He shook himself, no time to go off at tangents – he settled down for another hour's rest and then, feeling reasonably refreshed (he hadn't had a very successful night's hunt and so was a bit peckish) set off for Charlie's field.

His luck was in. There in the sunshine were Charlie, Hen and Black Hen and no sign of any Uprights who might make them wary.

He swooped over and settled on the fence rail.

"Good afternoon."

"Good afternoon," they chorused and then, as was customary they all allowed a little time to elapse- as was only polite.

Suddenly Owl spotted a large Newt scrambling across from the dyke, in plain view of them all. Foolish creature. Owl's juices started to flow at the mere sight of him and with no delay he swooped silently down, pounced on the unsuspecting Newt and swallowed him even before reaching his perch.

Ah – that was better. He ruffled his feathers and clacked his beak together in satisfaction.

"You shouldn't oughter do that," this from Hen of all animals.

"I beg your pardon," said Owl who was not used to being challenged on such matters.

"I said," repeated Hen, rather tetchily, "You shouldn't oughter do that."

"The 'ought to' is not required in that sentence Hen, it is incorrect grammar."

"Don't care," said Hen still scratching about, "You still oughtened not do that."

Owl sighed and gave up, " Why oughtened I to do that? It's what Owl's do. Hens eat worms don't they!" Good point he thought, top that!

Hen looked up beadily, "Because they are *in danger*."

"Well, they are certainly *in danger* if I'm about." he looked down at the little group, pleased with his pun.

"I think," said Black Hen, "She means, *endangered*."

"In danger, endangered, no odds," said Hen testily."

Owl and Charlie both looked rather bemused, and Owl said, "What are you two going on about?"

Black Hen ruffled her feathers and stood up, "Endangered Species are what Uprights say when they mean there aren't many of 'em. They worry about it. Remember that bit of paper that blew in some weeks back. It had a story about exactly that.

Mentioned some other things too but Newts figured largely in it. Uprights get very excited about Newts - don't quite know why."

She sat down and waited.

"Well," said Owl heavily, "I get pretty excited about Newts, but I agree that you don't see as many as you used to."

"That's 'cos you eat 'em," said Hen.

Owl looked a little abashed. He knew that Charlie and some other animals couldn't understand why one animal would eat another. Strictly speaking of course, he was a bird but in the animal world they tended to ignore unnecessary divisions. Sometimes he wondered why some like Horses and Cows, for example were happy just to eat grass and as for sheep – well they positively loved it and never seemed bored but then Sheep on the whole were a pretty dim lot.

They all fell silent for a while not wishing to make more of this small spat.

After a few minutes. Charlie said, "I remember that paper about the Newts. It said that some of the Uprights with yellow hats had been made to stop building a whole lot of those concrete boxes, houses, you know because they saw Newts in the field they were going to use."

"Really?" said Owl. "You mean that they would stop all that noise and mess and ruin that they love making just because of a Newt?"

"That's right," said Charlie, "Just like Hen said they are *in danger*."

"Endangered," said Black Hen.

Hen glared and with much ruffling and squawking she stalked back to their Hen House. "'So picky!' she thought, "It was me as told 'em. That's what they don't like." And she was right of course.

Charlie and Owl pondered this, "Do you think if we had more Newts they might stop putting up posters and planning things?" asked Charlie.

"Hm, my thoughts exactly," said Owl.

Black Hen coughed discreetly, "Of course, it does mean, Owl old chap, that you'd have to stop eating the little blighters."

Owl agreed but said "I would be willing to resist eating them if it would help, of course, but it's not easy to make much of a show of a Newt is it? I mean we'd be very lucky if anyone noticed the little blighters at all."

After a few minutes Black Hen said, "I suppose Hen could go and have a word with them. They trust her because she doesn't like to eat them, never has. I could ask her if she could have a chat, perhaps invite them over and tell them we could do with some help. It's a start and they must get pretty bored poking about in those ditches all day."

"It's a good suggestion," said Charlie "But," he hesitated and cleared his throat, "do you think Hen will get all that across to them ok, will she understand the plan?"

"And will she understand the Newts?" put in Owl, "They're tricky beggars to understand are Newts. I can't get the hang of their lingo at all, but then they don't hang about if they see me and they don't say much if I eat 'em either." Hen nodded wisely and agreed that they had a strange way of talking, more squeaks and sort of 'squishy' noises than words. "But Hen is a bird of few words herself and she seems to get on quite well with them," said Owl thoughtfully.

So it was agreed that Hen would make an initial approach to the Newts and report back to the others. She would go the next morning, early – no time to waste.

Hen was actually very pleased to be given this important task. After all, who else would communicate with them as well as she. Certainly not Owl who scared them witless and Horse would probably tread on them. She preened her feathers and ate some extra corn preparatory to spending time thinking about what she would say.

The next morning, at about 5.30, Hen got up, shook herself and peered out of the hen house door. Black hen was fast asleep and she wished she was too. Well, she had promised to go on this important mission and go she would. She set off across the field in the direction of the big pond with the overhanging tree which leant right over, trailing its topmost leaves in to the pond like someone washing their hair.

She hoped she was in time to catch one of the Newts on its way back to the pond. The Newts liked to go out and about at night and then snuggle in to a nice clump of weed or under a big stone in the cool and damp. Hen shivered, she never could see why creatures, including Owl liked to go out foraging for food at night. Hen liked the daytime, the activity, the chat and commotion of every day life. Anti-social way of carrying on. Still, each creature to its own.

Ah! Hen spotted a Smooth Newt making its rather weary way back to the pond.

"Good morning," she called out and the Newt, surprised, stopped and turned to see who had called out just as he was headed for home and his nice comfortable log by the edge of the pond.

"Ah," he squished, "Morning Hen. Haven't seen you for a while."

"Been a bit busy lately," she replied.

Hen was far more relaxed when chatting with Newts. She actually had quite a good vocabulary but when she talked to Charlie, or particularly Owl she tended to feel nervous and inadequate (or would have done if she had known what *inadequate* meant). Owl talked so fast and became impatient if she took too long to think of her words. He would make that curious hissing sound through his beak and she knew that this was his way of suppressing his instinct to screech, he was, after all, a screech owl.

"I wanted to talk to you about something quite important which could upset our lives and homes. We are trying to get a sort of 'Action for Animals' group together and would like you to join and help us."

She sat down on the grass to recover her breath after such a long sentence. At least now she had the full attention of the Newt and she proceeded to tell him all about the Planning Application and the ideas that they had come up with.

"So you see Newt, we really need your help as you are *endangered* as Owl says and Charlie and Owl would like a meeting with you. Oh please help us, you and your friends. You were the first ones we thought of and we want to get all sorts of other *in danger* creatures to join our group too."

She looked pleadingly at Newt but she needn't have worried. The risk that their beautiful pond might be destroyed was quite enough to get him interested.

"I believe," said Newt, "That Uprights only get upset about particular sorts of Newts."

Now this was news to Hen, "What particular sorts of Newts? Aren't you all more or less the same?" Really she thought, this is starting to get complicated.

"You see Hen, I am an everyday sort of chap. No airs and graces, you get what you see. But some of us are a bit different. Now, take the Great Crested Newt, we have a few in our pond you know, quite a distinction. They're bigger than us and when it gets to (he paused and coughed discreetly) a certain time of the year, do you follow me Hen?"

"No," said Hen.

"Look here Hen, I can't shilly-shally, I mean the breeding season!"

"Oh, of course Newt," she said, not wanting to appear silly, "I know all about that." She didn't of course!

Newt sighed, "Well anyhow, these big rare chaps get very excited, het up you know. Quite a nuisance really, crashing about the place, showing off and bragging and they grow these big spiky sort of crests on their backs. Can't think how. I tried once, didn't work at all. They get sort of brighter colours too and a stripe."

"A stripe!" exclaimed Hen.

"I know, I know, it's all very daft anyhow, they do. Now the Uprights love these big spiky chaps and they also like the smaller ones with sort of webbed back feet- Palmate or that's what they said when I went to school."

Hen was beginning to feel quite dizzy. Out of her depth. But she felt she must continue and complete her task.

"Personally," said Newt. "If I see a pretty Newt that takes my fancy I just go over, introduce myself and before you know it-

Bob's your Uncle!" He puffed out his chest and his eyes glazed over for a second. Suddenly he started to laugh.

A Newt's laugh is hard to describe but it is a mixture of wheezing, fizzing and popping in a squishy sort of way. He looked so funny that Hen started to laugh as well. I do like Newts she thought. I never laugh like this with Charlie and Owl or Black Hen for that matter.

"Now," said Newt, suddenly becoming serious, "What you need is to get this over to the Special Ones. Us common Newts are all very well, but the Uprights won't be all that bothered about us. Leave it with me and I'll speak to them this evening, before we set out. I'm sure they'll want to join the Group and I'll ask a couple of them to go over and see Charlie and Owl.

"But," he said, suddenly struck by a thought, "They won't come near unless Owl promises absolutely not to eat any of them. If he does that, the deal's off!"

Hen reassured Newt that this point had already been discussed and Owl had promised that on no account would he eat anybody engaged in helping to save their lives and homes.

"Good," said Newt, letting out an enormous yawn, "Now I must go and get some sleep. Leave it to me and as soon as we've talked about it, a couple of the Special ones will come over and see you and Black Hen at your house. We'll only go in to Charlie's field with you two at first anyway. We have to trust Owl."

Hen agreed and thanked Newt for his time. She knew he must be tired and she could do no more for now. She left him and went back to her house where Black Hen was just stirring. She flopped on to the straw and decided that before she did any more talking she must have a jolly good sleep.

Black Hen looked at Hen and, although bursting to know how she had got on with the Newts, she crept quietly out in to the morning air so as not to disturb her. She had earned her rest.

Black Hen contented herself with pecking about by the hen house, sipping some water and biding her time.

At last Hen awoke, and with the satisfied feeling of a job well done and a weight off her mind she got up and went out to see Black Hen. The two spent quite some time scratching around near each other, chatting away and stopping occasionally to sit down at any important bits of the previous day's meeting. Black Hen had not realised that there were different types of Newts and that some mattered to Uprights more than others. She listened with interest, her head cocked on one side, beady eyes bright and fixed on Hen until she had finished her tale.

"And so," said Hen at last, "The Special Newts will come to us and we will accompany them to Owl and Charlie. They don't fully trust Owl you see."

Black Hen nodded and stood up, "Well done Hen, a really first class job."

Hen, who didn't often get praise, fluffed up her feathers and muttered, "Oh, it was nothing really, just want to do my bit you know."

"Now," said Black Hen, "Would you like me to go and see Charlie and Owl and pass this on or would you like to do it yourself?"

"Oh, please go for me Black Hen. You know Charlie is fine, but Owl will get impatient and glare at me and all my words will just run away!"

"Very well my friend, you have done quite enough for now. I'll pop over and see them."

Hen, with a sigh of relief, went back up the little ramp in to the house and settled down to think things over.

Owl wants to go to bed.

5. OWL GETS CROSS, but not for long

Needless to say Owl was waiting anxiously on the top fence rail. He wanted to go to bed but knew that he would never sleep until the Hens had reported back to him. He clawed his way back and forth along the rail making small hissing sounds through his beak. When he saw Black Hen approaching he forgot himself altogether and let out a loud SCREEEECH! This made Charlie jump and Black Hen stopped dead in her tracks.

"Steady on old fellow," said Charlie, "Keep your feathers on."

"Sorry, sorry my friends, I'm a little tense you know. Where is Hen?"

"I've spoken to her this morning, had a full report and she has done extremely well. She spoke to a Smooth Newt, Common Newt you know, and he said we need to speak to the Special Newts as they are the ones that Uprights get most excited about."

"SPECIAL NEWTS!" exploded Owl, "Who said anything about SPECIAL NEWTS!"

"Hen told me all about them and she is quite right, we do need to see them."

"Where are they then?" screeched Owl, "I see no Newts, special or otherwise. I see it all, Hen has messed up. She's allowed herself to fobbed off, she should never have been trusted with so important a job."

He flapped his wings a few times and then settled back on to the rail and glared at Black Hen.

"Now, now old chap," this from Charlie who had sauntered over to the fence, "Don't get so het up. If Black Hen says Hen has done well, then she has and I think we must show our appreciation. Apart from anything else it is bad manners to mistrust a friend like Hen. It simply isn't done in animal circles."

Owl had the grace to look rather ashamed and hissed through his beak, "Sorry, sorry, forgot myself."

They said no more about the outburst.

"So when are these 'SPECIAL NEWTS' coming to see us. We've no time to lose you know. "

Black Hen cleared her throat and said, "You see Owl, they don't altogether feel safe with you seeing as how you sometimes eat them. Hen did explain that you had agreed that you would leave them strictly alone, but they wish to come with us, altogether, for safety you see."

Now Owl really did look ashamed. It seemed that he was the reason for any delay, not Hen and he looked quite humbly at Black Hen and asked, "When did she say they might come?"

"Tomorrow very early, on their way back to the pond."

"Suits me," said Owl.

Charlie looked up, "And me, I'll get up as soon as I hear you all about. What about language though? Will we understand them?"

"Hen says that if you are very patient, she fixed Owl with a beady eye, and listen quietly you will hear enough words amongst all the squishing and fizzing to know what they are on about."

With that Black Hen turned on her heel and marched over towards the Hen House, Charlie sauntered over to the water bowser for a long drink and Owl, rose thankfully in to the air and sailed off to the barn for a good long sleep.

The next morning Owl was perched on an old tree stump which was lower than his usual place on the top fence rail. He felt this might make him appear less intimidating to the Newts. Charlie was standing quite near to Owl and had positioned himself carefully so that he had no need to move until the meeting was over. One *clomp* of a big hoof would be a terrible danger to an unwary Newt and Charlie understood how important it was not to kill any of them.

Hen and Black Hen were waiting by the hen house for the arrival of the Newts and before long.

Owl, with his keen eyesight said, "Here they come Charlie, just crawling under the fence, can you see them?"

Charlie looked, and after a few seconds, when they were a bit nearer he too could make them out. They were quite an entourage. At the head of the group was a particularly large Great Crested Newt. He had very striking markings and crawled with quite a high stepping gait (for a Newt). He was flanked by Hen on one side and Black Hen on the other. Beside the Hens were two further Crested Newts, and behind them some slightly smaller ones, who Owl presumed were the Palmate Newts with the webbed back feet. He couldn't for the life of him think why Uprights should get het up about these smaller Newts.

"Dammit all," he thought, "You can't even see their feet, webbed or otherwise so what's all the fuss?"

Surrounding the Special Newts was a semi circle of Common Smooth Newts.

"Altogether quite a showing," thought Owl, "have to admire their spirit."

The two Great Crested Newts behind the leader had dark blodges round their eyes and they were constantly looking around checking the area, rather like the C.I.A. agents that you see in dark sunglasses behind Presidents and other important Uprights. Of course, impressive though this was, both Owl and Charlie were aware that in five seconds flat, he could eat 'em all or Charlie could flatten them!

"Good morning," said Owl and Charlie, "Thank you for coming to see us."

The lead Newt answered something like this, "Squelch, fizz. we greet, pop, wheeze, squelch, you, pop."

As Hen had said, you could indeed catch the odd word but it needed great patience and concentration, which were not Owl's forte. Nonetheless, the meeting continued. Owl set out the general plan and the importance of the Newts being able to appear in force, with very short notice, once the animals knew a date for an Official Upright's visit.

After a bit of negotiation regarding some tricky details and a long reassurance from Owl that he would not eat any of them, they came to an agreement. Hen had played an invaluable part as translator, with Black Hen's assistance when she found Owl too scary.

With a final speech consisting almost entirely of fizzing and squishing, the Newts retreated and made their way back to the pond. It had been arranged that come the hour when they were needed, Hen would rush over and find them, even if they had to be woken up and dragged out from their various stones and tree roots.

Owl rose thankfully up on to his fence rail and Charlie had a quick trot around the field to get the circulation back in his legs. The hens, once they had left the Newts to their pond and sleep, returned to the Hen House and settled down for a chat and then a well-deserved nap.

6. OWL'S GREAT DILEMMA

Once the Newts were *under their belts* so to speak, the Action Group settled down for a day or so and then started to discuss their next plan of action.

Quite late one afternoon when Owl had appeared a little early after a good day's sleep and Charlie was feeling quite lively after a short canter to the Hen House and back they fell in to mulling over their next move.

The two Hens had arrived, sensing something important in the air and pecked around casually within earshot of Owl and Charlie.

"What do you think we should go for next?" asked Owl.

"I think Bats are a good idea," said Charlie.

"Bats!" said Owl, looking a bit shifty, "Bats are all very well, but the main thing with Bats is that once they make a home somewhere the Uprights can't get 'em out! They are protected, BY LAW!" he added dramatically.

"Well," said Charlie, "That's perfect isn't it? For example if they move in to your barn, in the opposite corner. Of course," he added quickly, sensing an agitation in Owl, "then they couldn't knock down your barn could they? The Uprights I mean."

"But Charlie. My barn, MY barn!" his voice rose to a screech of anguish, "I like my privacy, the peace and quiet, the calm."

"Bats ain't noisy fellows," said Charlie.

"Ah, but you don't know," said Owl. "I used to live down in Devon for a while, nice countryside you know, very pretty but some Bats moved in to the neighbourhood and came to roost quite near me in an old abandoned cottage. You may think they are quiet but they chatter on in the evenings before they settle and they've got these silly, squeaky little voices. Most irritating. Gives you the pip.

"I left 'em to it and came up here, he continued," I'm still friendly with one or two of them, had a letter a couple of weeks back saying they'd quite like to come up to Norfolk for a holiday, but I didn't encourage them. They've even got a few of those ones the Uprights get worried about—Horseshoe Bats, queer looking chaps, very odd shaped noses. Devon's ideal for them, plenty of moths and beetles to eat, they're very fond of moths and beetles."

He drifted off slightly, gazing into the distance and remembering some balmy Devon days with a particularly pretty young Owl who'd taken a shine to him.

"Well, "said Black Hen who'd crept nearer and nearer until she was part of the conversation, "How about Dormice? They're very *in danger* we might be able to come up with one or two of those to approach. You must see them when you're out and about at night Owl. I know you are rather partial to eating them but hang it all old chap, if you don't want Bats 'cos they're noisy then it'll have to be Dormice!"

Charlie nodded, this was fair comment, "Yes, Owl," he said, "How about it?"

They looked up at Owl who appeared to have grown to about twice his normal size. He was edging back and forth on the fence rail, whistling and clacking his beak angrily.

"Rather partial to a Dormouse, rather partial! They are my absolute favourite treat and not so easy to come by either. You'd never get a Dormouse to believe I wouldn't eat it because I would! So there! Stick that in your Horse Box Charlie and see how you like it."

Now this was very rude of Owl. Charlie was very proud of his home or his *trailer* as he sometimes called it in a more casual moment. At no time did he or anyone else refer to it as his *Horse Box*!

The very idea! As if he was some stupid little pony performing for the Uprights and at the mercy of them towing him about willy-nilly.

Owl knew he had gone too far and of course it was his undoing. He shuffled about a bit more, turned round and round on his perch once or twice, but he knew he was beat.

An animal insulting another animal, particularly with reference to his home, be it a tiny nest or a huge Badger's Sett was completely out of order. The height of bad manners. He felt ashamed and said, "I beg your pardons, all of you." He turned his flat face round to the hens who were looking up at the sky and pretending they had not noticed this shocking breach of etiquette.

They looked up at Owl and then at Charlie who, being the easy going fellow he was, quickly overlooked the insult and said to Owl, "There, there Owl, don't worry, no offence taken. Understand you are under a lot of stress at the moment and, after all, you've been very good about giving up eating Newts."

Owl sighed with relief and said to Charlie, "Thank you, I have felt stressed and after all an Owl's got to live you know, got to keep body and soul together.

"I can't give up the Dormice but I will get in touch with my Bat friends in Devon and invite them up, see if they'll help us you know. They are quite an amiable lot, don't know why the Uprights get so scared of them. I'll write to them tonight before I set out. Only hope they won't want to stay for too long." he added rather sadly.

Black Hen looked beadily at Hen, who was trying to hide the fact that she was crying in to a tuft of grass (she was a soft hearted creature) and felt sorry for Owl even though he scared her.

"Hm, hm," she coughed, "I have a thought Owl. Why not offer them a short term lease, make a proper Animal's agreement you know."

Animal's agreements were legally binding and did not need writing down. "Do you think they would do that?"

Owl brightened and straightened his back, "Bats do love a barn and you don't get them so much nowadays. I told them about mine, boasting a bit I suppose," he said sheepishly. "They thought it sounded just the place for a visit. What do you all think? Shall we try for Bats next?"

Well, of course, they all agreed because apart from Bats being a sure fire bet on the *endangered* front, it let Owl off the hook with his Dormice.

It had been a close run thing but they had avoided breaking up the Animal's Action Group and despite one rather fierce spat had avoided losing their friendships which mattered so much to them all.

Hen wiped away the last of her tears on some grass stalks, Owl flew back to E1693340 to consider his letter and Charlie, still nursing a bit of hurt about the 'horse box' comment lay down and had a good roll in the dry dust at the edge of the field until he felt better.

Time for the bats to arrive

7   BATS

A couple of weeks elapsed before Owl received an answer to his letter. They had all become rather anxious during this time and Owl had pecked off two further planning application posters and ripped them in to shreds, some of which he had used to plump up the bedding in the Box.

When the reply came he wasted no time but, having read it carefully aloud for Mrs Owl's benefit, he spent several minutes calming her down and stopping her from fretting about, "Making up beds," and "What part of our lovely Barn will they take over?"

On and on she went marching round the box, planning lists of good hunting areas and generally working herself up in to quite a state, pecking at her feathers and leaving little wisps of them in her wake.

"Now, now my dear," they were very fond of each other, "You are upsetting yourself over nothing. I know these chaps quite well and they will have no problem settling in and finding the best places to *hang out*. I have to work out the terms of the Animals' Agreement and I can't hear myself think with you flapping about and getting in a state. Smooth out your feathers my love and have a chew on this last bit of Shrew, fresh last night you know."

Mrs Owl was aware that Owl had been saving this little titbit for himself and felt rather ashamed for carrying on so, it didn't stop her from eating the Shrew though, she was a bird of good appetite and Owl liked to see her sleek and plump.

"I'm sorry Owl," she chased the last little bit of fur round her beak, "I just worry that they will be noisy or difficult and spoil our quiet little life here."

"I know my love but there's plenty of room in this barn and they'll stick to the lease I'm sure. Honourable fellows, Bats, besides it is important you know to get as many creatures on our side as we can to join the Action Group."

They nuzzled close to each other and pecked softly, making little noises of affection.

Once Owl had settled Mrs Owl he re-read the letter and decided that even though he felt quite tired after his night's hunting, he had better see if he could gather the others together for a meeting, the Bats were coming soon.

He flew swiftly over to the fence rail and looked around the field. Good, there was dependable Charlie, grazing quietly in the morning sun. He couldn't see all the Hens, but there was Black Hen pecking around near the Hen House. No sign of Hen and Slippers.

For a moment he thought, "Does it really matter if they are not here? They can always be filled in later."

Then, he felt ashamed. Good and loyal creatures that they were, of course they must be included and have their say, "We are in this together!" he said aloud.

The Bat's writing was not too hard to make out, it was rather as they speak. He felt that it was 'squeaky' writing. "It was," as he said to Charlie, "Small and oddly spaced with lots of ticks and dots strewn randomly about the page.

Charlie listened with interest. He had become quite anxious waiting for the letter but didn't want to let on to Owl in case it seemed like a criticism of his friend and this, of course, would never do.

"They say," said Owl importantly, "They have been thinking of having a little jaunt up to Norfolk, do a spot of hunting, have a look at the countryside and so on. Very grateful they are too for the offer of lodging in the barn for a while. They agree to the short term lease and will stay beyond that time if required, in order to defeat the Upright's plans."

"Of course," he added, "They are well versed in such matters as beating Planning Applications, even stopping building work after it's started! They don't tiptoe around you know. Stubborn as you like, got the unions on their side too."

Charlie liked the sound of this and got Owl to repeat it to Black Hen, Hen and even Slippers, to be sure they all knew the plan.

"When do they say they might come?" asked Black Hen.

"Oh quite soon, perhaps in the next 2 or 3 days."

This threw Hen and Slippers in to quite a panic.

"Aren't Bats terribly scary?" asked Slippers trembling slightly as she spoke.

"Not so," said Owl, peering kindly down at the Hens, "Best of fellows. You mustn't go by all you read you know."

"Huh!" said Slippers, immediately insulted at the suggestion that she should read at all, though she could.

"Some of us," she squawked, "Have better things to do than lie about reading bits of paper. There's plants to peck up and worms to pull and anyhow, I aint stupid," Slipper's grammar tended to go wrong if she got offended.

Charlie clomped slowly over to the Hens and snuffling softly through his nostrils said, "No one is saying anyone is stupid, that would be terribly rude and not true at all. Why we wouldn't have got this far if Hen hadn't helped us with the Newts would we?"

By appealing gently to the Hens they immediately softened and enjoyed the flattery.

"Sorry," they said in unison to Charlie though they ignored Owl, "Think we'll go back to our House and have a rest. These are very trying times you know."

"Indeed they are," thought Charlie, "I'm just as worried as the Hens really, but it doesn't help to show it. We must stay united or we'll lose the fight."

To his surprise, the very next day Owl received another letter from the Bats saying that they were planning to arrive that evening!

He felt a mixture of surprise, joy and panic all together. Suppressing the panic he concentrated on the facts.

He must call an extraordinary meeting of the Animals' Action Group without delay. He swooped over to Charlie's field and called him. Charlie sauntered over, chewing absently at the tougher grasses near the fence. Owl spotted Black Hen and called to her to fetch Hen and Slippers to join them by the fence.

Owl screeched fairly gently to draw attention to his presence. He felt slightly nervous because, apart from the important announcement about the Bats, he had another news item to share.

When they were all present he coughed, shifted his claws about on the rail and turned round once or twice.

They looked up at Owl expectantly, "Ahem, thank you for coming, I have some important news for you. In fact two important items."

They all waited. "Well," said Hen, "spit it out!"

"I . . . ," he cleared his throat, "I mean, we are . . . ," he gave a low screech and clacked his beak, "That is to say . . . , Mrs Owl is expecting another brood of young'uns."

He looked down at his feet. He always found the sharing of quite such personal news rather embarrassing but it was necessary to tell them, because, apart from anything else, Mrs Owl could become, shall we say, a lttle aeriated at such times, a little tetchy and he needed the others to make allowances.

They were all well aware of Mrs Owl's mood changes and to be honest they found it quite amusing to watch Owl's efforts to cover up for her.

"Many congratulations Owl" said Charlie and the others all squawked, "Here, here!"

"Thanks awfully," muttered Owl, "I'll pass your messages on to Mrs Owl."

"What is the other piece of news then?" asked Black Hen beadily.

"The Bats are coming this evening!"

My goodness you might as well have thrown a bomb in to the field! Charlie reared up on his hind legs and neighed, Black Hen did the Hen equivalent of punching the air, whatever that might be, and the other two Hens ran about squawking and pecking and generally bumping in to everybody.

"What time?"

"How many?"

"Will they go straight to the barn?" the questions came thick and fast.

"Calm down, calm down now everyone. I think they will be very tired. They've had to hunt on the wing while travelling long distances. Not much sleep you know. It's very good of them to leave their home comforts to come and support us."

They all nodded and talked amongst themselves.

"This is an important thing for us. The Bats are serious fellows, they've overturned many Uprights' plans and know a lot of stuff that will be helpful to us. I suppose they will turn up around dusk or maybe even the next morning, early. We shall just have to keep our eyes peeled and get naps here and there during the day as best we can."

Owl had said quite enough for one speech and without further comment, swooped off to the barn and Mrs Owl. The others straggled back to their homes to rest but spent quite a lot of time, chatting and calling out to each other. Hen said that later on she would stroll over to the pond and let the Newts know what was happening.

Eventually, as the sun rose in the sky, peace came to their little world and, on and off, they dozed.

The Bats didn't arrive until quite late in the evening, there was still a faint haze of light but the last glimmerings of dusk were fading.

It was Charlie who spotted them first. He had looked up in to the sky, as they'd all been doing during the evening and thought, "Ah, getting darker now, looks like a black cloud coming over by the pond, that won't help."

Then he suddenly realised that it wasn't a cloud but a small colony of Bats approaching from the south-west. He trotted over to the fence but Owl must have popped out for a quick swoop over the fields in search of prey. No sign of the Hens and he wasn't too keen on disturbing them because, Hen and Slippers would get in the most fearful state of excitement which tended to make things worse.

He shook back his mane, gave a few snorts and then a fairly loud whinny. The Bats swooped low over his field as if to say, "Hello, we have arrived!" and then rose up as one and flew straight in through the high barn doorway.

"Well," thought Charlie, "I know they are good at finding things in the dark, but I had thought that Owl would be here to show them in. Decisive fellows, just what we need!" Then, he suddenly thought of Mrs Owl and knew that on his return Owl would be in big trouble!

The Bats meantime had poured in to the barn and spied Owl's box - E1693340 in the far corner. No sign of Owl so they proceeded to make themselves at home. They took up the two opposite corners, high in the old rafters and hung themselves upside down in quiet rows, after a bit of jostling for position.

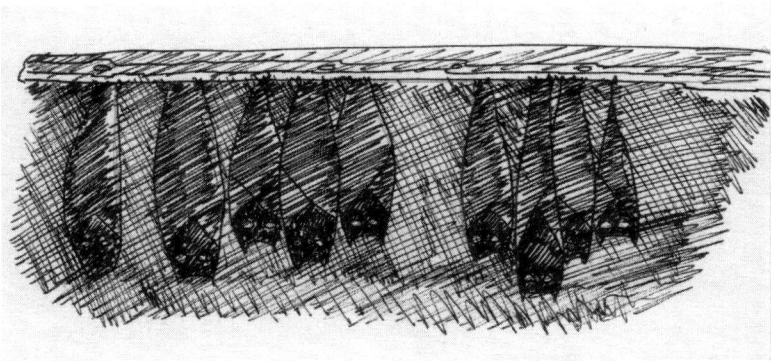

The only obvious sign that they were there was their beady little eyes, caught by a shaft of moonlight which had found a hole in the old, tiled roof; tiny pin points of light sprinkled around the rafters as they settled to rest after their long journey.

Mrs Owl had not heard their silent entry but sensed some sort of gentle commotion as they settled, and so she poked her wary head out of the box hole and peered around.

"Was it Owl?" she wondered, "And if so what on earth was he up to, why hadn't he come in?"

At first she saw nothing and then, as her eyes adjusted, spotted the little beady, blinking pin-points of light.

She withdrew her head quickly. What to do, what to do? What could it mean? And then, she suddenly realised that it must be the Bats! She poked her head out again and rotating the flat disc of her face from left to right she gradually made out the outlines of rows of soft little bodies hanging neatly side-by-side.

"And where was Owl?" she asked the air. "All that fuss and speechifying and puffing up his feathers and now, just when he was needed, he was out enjoying himself, feasting and chatting to passers by in the fields and woods."

'Typical," she said to herself, "Just like an owl, they're all the same, leaving their mates to do all the real work!"

She went on like this for a little while, marching round the box, kicking up straw and bits of torn up planning applications as she went.

It suddenly occurred to her that this was actually a very good opportunity for her to shine. So she slipped out of the hole and, staying very much to her side of the barn, flew out and over to Charlie's field.

"Ah!" said Charlie, much surprised by Mrs Owl's appearance, "Good evening Mrs Owl, how are you feeling? Can I help you?"

"Good evening Charlie," she said calmly, fluttering down on to the top rail of the fence, "No, no thank you, I am fine and need no help. I am just reporting to you that the Bats are all here and I've settled them in to their homes in the barn, this of course was rather stretching the truth. They seem pleasant enough. Having a rest and then I expect they'll go out and explore.

"Will you tell Owl, if he happens to turn up, to come home quietly when he does return," this was said rather pointedly, "as, I and perhaps the Bats, will be asleep. We have had rather a busy time you know!"

"Certainly Mrs Owl," said a puzzled Charlie. He wasn't used to Mrs Owl being calm and practical. Perhaps, this was how expecting another brood was taking her this time instead of squawking hysterically around and giving Owl such a hard time. He hoped it would last but something about her tone of voice and a look in her eye made him feel it wouldn't.

The Bats proved to be very self sufficient and during their stay in the Barn were so quiet and orderly that after a few weeks it was easy to forget they were there at all. Initially, of course, they had to meet up with Owl and also, Black Hen, Hen and Slippers. They were not agreeable to appearing in broad daylight in Charlie's field and so it was arranged that the Animals' Action Group would go to them in the Barn. Unfortunately this excluded Charlie who wasn't able to get out of his field, unless he jumped the fence which would be far too dramatic and hardly discreet. Anyhow, he wasn't all that sure that he could manage it nowadays and he didn't in the least mind missing out on the Bat visit.

The little group of Hens went warily over to the Barn at dusk. Black Hen led the way and Slippers came last. Owl was already perched on a handy rafter near to the bats who, in the main, hung in soft and silent rows.

"How unnerving," thought Black Hen but she said nothing to frighten the others.

There seemed to be a small, separate cluster of bats, two of whom seemed rather different to the others. When you looked more closely (or as close as you dared) their faces seemed oddly misshapen with strange noses rather like curled up leaves set in a leathery curve. Horseshoe Bats! Black Hen had heard of these but thought that they only lived in the West Country. How good of them to come all this way.

The two Horseshoe Bats were flanked on either side by the Common Bats and seemed to behave rather like the A-List celebrities with their minders which the Uprights liked to watch and report on in their papers. They preened and posed and had bagged the most comfortable position in the rafters. The Common Bats were quite in awe of them despite their rather off-putting appearance.

Owl duly introduced the Hens, Mrs Owl, who poked her head out of the Box, nodded and then disappeared, and himself and made a very good little speech of welcome and thanks.

It took a little time to explain their mission and how it would work and it was hard to tell if the Bats approved, or even if they had heard, so silent and unmoving were they hanging in their rows.

At last the larger Horseshoe Bat thanked Owl for his greetings and the excellent Barn accommodation. He explained that although his Common Bat friends would stay for the duration of the lease, he and his companion would be heading back to Devon after the 'Big Day' when the Surveyor and his helpers would come to assess the fields. He was at pains to make them understand the very great honour that they had bestowed on Owl and his little group by having come at all. They wished to support the cause and lend their expertise in such situations but then the Devon fields and hills would call and they would have to leave.

All the creatures understood this feeling and could relate to it. They duly thanked the Horseshoe and all the other Bats again and were about to leave when the Head Bat asked,

"And how shall we know when we are needed to appear? When is the Big Day?"

Owl explained that they did not precisely know but the posters had been up for some weeks (except when Owl tore them down and shredded them) and as soon as there was any activity, he personally would inform them immediately. This seemed to satisfy them and at some unseen and unheard signal, they swished from the rafters in a soft, dark cloud, streamed through the Barn door and off in to the night.

Owl retreated to his Box and the others to the Hen House and the next morning as Owl returned from his night's hunting, he called in and told Charlie about the meeting.

Robin waits for instructions.

8   MAKING PLANS

"Course," said Charlie, "they have a point. I mean come the day we will need to let everyone know as quick as we can so they can get over here. Could be tricky. I can't go and the Hens are very willing but not very fast. What do you think Owl?"

Owl pondered for a minute and then said "I have thought about this, particularly if we manage to get a few more animals on board. I wondered what you thought about asking Robin to help?"

Now this was a clever idea. Mr Robin, of course, didn't live with them as the others did but he visited several times a day, looked in at the Hens, pecked about a bit and then flew off to his own territory in a field several hedgerows away from theirs.

He didn't often see Owl because of Owl's nocturnal habits but they had exchanged the occasional greeting. He was a cheery, helpful sort of bird and might well agree to be a sort of *on call* messenger.

"I mean I can tell the Bats and Hen will go and see the Newts but once we start enlisting others to our group we may need to look further afield. Do you think, Charlie, that you could have a chat with Black Hen and see if she will discuss it with Robin?"

"Certainly," said Charlie, nodding his head slowly.

Neither creature had noticed that Robbie had brought out the Hairy Upright for an early morning walk and that they had paused to look in at them. The Hairy Upright had his arms folded on the top of the gate and Robbie peered through the bars below. Because he was a peaceful fellow, he and Robbie made no sound and as they watched the two creatures deep in discussion.

The Hairy Upright thought that they looked for all the world as if they are cooking something up. A few tattered remains of the latest planning application poster, were drifting about the field in the light breeze and one of them had caught on the fence rail. He and Robbie looked at this and again at the pair by the trailer and then Robbie took The Hairy Upright away, "Hm!" they both thought in unison.

When Robin was approached and understood the dilemma he was very willing to act as a messenger. He could be swift and accurate and knew the whereabouts of most of the creatures nearby. In fact, he had made rather a good suggestion of his own regarding a new addition to Group.

Black Hen told Owl and Charlie one evening, "Robin suggested Hedgehogs! There aren't nearly as many as there used to be, we've all noticed that and Uprights are very fond of Hedgehogs."

"True, true," nodded Owl and Charlie.

"But," said Charlie, "They're rather tricky chaps, don't you think. I mean they spend most of their time rolled up in balls. Never understand why. Do they think they can't be seen if they do that? How do we communicate with something that stays rolled up in a ball?"

Owl paced up and down on his rail and gave a few soft screeches. The night and the fields were beginning to call him and he longed to be off but this idea needed some thought.

"Tell you what old boy, ask Black Hen to look in to it. One of those Hens may have come across the odd Hedgehog when they are scratching about by the dykes. See what she says and get back to me."

Charlie knew that it was time for Owl to leave and was not at all disturbed when Owl suddenly stretched his gleaming wings and floated away in to the distance. He would talk to Black Hen tomorrow and she could talk to the others.

"Really," he thought, "it is all quite exhausting. I can hardly remember the days when I just grazed and drank and cantered about a bit, it's all go now." But actually he was quite enjoying the excitement and it stopped him worrying about his home.

9 A PRICKLY PROBLEM FOR SLIPPERS

Next day Black Hen waited until the other two Hens were up and about and then asked them to have a talk with her over by the Hen House. They settled down in the shade and Black Hen told them all about the Hedgehog plan.

"Not sure how to go about it," she said, "After all, as soon as they catch sight of anyone they roll up into a ball! Can you imagine if we did that, or Owl or Charlie!"

Unexpectedly, Slippers spoke first, "Actually, I used to know a couple of Hedgehogs a bit. They lived over there." She indicated with her beak, "Amongst the hedgerow by the dyke. Used to find them pottering about sometimes and stopped for a chat."

"You mean," said Hen, "they didn't roll up?"

"Oh they rolled up alright, straight away, soon as they saw me coming."

"Well," said Black Hen exasperatedly, "How could you talk to them?"

"Well, you just does! I used to sit down beside them and talk quietly and they would answer. They didn't unroll, or very rarely, but it hardly mattered. Their voices were muffled, bit like talking to someone buried in the middle of a haystack!"

This made them cackle with laughter.

When they had settled down again Black Hen asked, "Do you think you could go and see if they're still about. Even if it isn't them there might be some others there. What do you think?"

Rather like Hen with the Newts, Slippers, who was unused to being given anything of importance, or even anything at all, to do, preened her feathery feet and said casually, "Oh yes, no problem, I'll wander around later and see what I find."

About two-ish, after a short nap, Slippers shuffled away over to the dyke and walked along the edge for quite some way, looking in amongst the Hawthorn and Elder and Old Man's Beard which grew thickly here. By the time she spotted a Hedgehog, nosing about under the long grass she was even more speckled than usual as she was liberally coated with the seeds and pollen of the Old Man's Beard.

"Afternoon Hedgehog," she called. The hedgehog looked up and immediately rolled into a tight ball. There he lay, perfectly still. The only sign of life being his little spiky sides, puffing in and out quite fast.

Slippers sat down and in a conversational tone said, "Please don't worry. My name is Slippers and I am a Bantam - a rather fine one actually," she added modestly, "I used to chat to you fellows, months ago. Don't suppose you were one of them were you?"

After a pause, the Hedgehog said in muffled tones, "Not me, but one of my friends mentioned you by name."

Slippers swelled with pride. Imagine being 'known' in the Hedgehog community. This would show the others.

"I've come on behalf of our little group over in Charlie the Horse's field and Owl in the Barn."

She didn't mention Bats, this seemed like too much all at once.

"What do you want?" This from the depths of the spiky ball.

Slippers sat closer (but not too close to the spines) and started to explain. She waited and began to think the Hedgehog had gone to sleep but then noticed that slowly and cautiously he was starting to unroll. What an honour! She took pains to sit very still and wait patiently.

At last, Hedgehog managed to unroll completely and a fine big animal he was. He turned to Slippers and looked straight in to her beady eyes. As she looked back in to his, which were soft and bright and gentle, she felt a strange warm, melty feeling coming over her. It sorted of started at her toes and then spread all through her middle. Most odd, she had never felt that before.

Hedgehog continued to look in to her eyes and thought, "What a pretty little bird, so soft and speckly and small." He felt he would like to look after her.

Neither spoke at first and then Hedgehog asked, "How would we know when you wanted us to come?"

"If there is time I would come myself but if it was urgent then Robin said he would come over and find one of you. I think you know Robin don't you, he lives in the field on the other side of road but he visits us every day or two and he said he'd come more often for now."

Hedgehog liked the sound of this, and he liked the look of Slippers too.

They agreed that he should come over to Charlie's field and meet the others for a chat and he said that was fine and that he and his friends were also scared that the Uprights seemed to be using more and more of their haunts and byways for those horrible boxes full of Uprights that they seemed to like so much.

At last, reluctantly, they parted with the agreement that Slippers would come over the next day and escort him over to meet the others.

Slippers kindly said "Feel free to roll up in to a ball if you wish, I've explained to them that they can still talk to you quite easily."

As she started to shuffle back she glanced behind her once at Hedgehog who was still unrolled and looking steadily after her.

Slippers felt herself trembling slightly and felt all melted again. Could this be falling in love she wondered. Is it alright to fall in love with a hedgehog if you are a Bantam? Oh dear, this was most confusing. She almost wished that she hadn't been asked to go but then such a warm, squashy feeling came over her that she thought "I'm glad I went," and then said out loud, "I'll ask Charlie."

Charlie, all innocence, was waiting for Slipper's return expecting to discuss her visit and how it had gone. When Slippers appeared and went over to him he obligingly lay down on the warm ground so that they could have a proper chat. Slippers sat by Charlie's long, soft head and sighed heavily.

"Is something wrong? Couldn't you talk to him? I wondered if it might be a problem."

"No, no problem like that. It went well and he is going to come over tomorrow. I'll go and get him so he can meet the Action Group. He's quite keen.

"I do have a problem though Charlie and I wondered if you could help."

"Strange," thought Charlie, "She does look a bit ruffled. Hope he wasn't rude to her. Surely not. If he was then he and Owl would give Hedgehog a piece of their minds when he came to see them."

Slippers scratched about a bit and turned in a few circles before sitting down again. Charlie's big soft eyes looked at her and gave her courage.

"It's like this Charlie. Hedgehog was very nice, he didn't know me from before but he knew my name from some of the others." Even though flustered she still swelled a bit when she said this.

Charlie interrupted to say, "Well done Slippers!"

"Anyhow," she said, not wanting to be interrupted, "The thing is, I mean to say, oh hang it Charlie, have you ever been in love?"

Well, you could have knocked Charlie down with a feather, though it would have to be a very, very large one, "In love!" he shouted.

Slippers looked round agitatedly, "Don't shout," she cried, "I don't want anyone to hear."

"Sorry Slippers but, if you don't mind me asking, what has me being in love got to do with anything?"

"Please Charlie," begged Slippers, "I need your help. Have you?"

Charlie puffed out his soft lips and blew down his nostrils quietly. "I'm not sure I know about *in love*. There was a pretty little filly I met years ago when I was younger and I suppose she made me feel a bit, well, excited and melted all at the same time but that's all I can think of."

"Yes, yes, " cried Slippers, "That's just how I feel, but I feel it for a Hedgehog, not a Bantam."

Charlie looked startled, got quickly to his feet and trotted round his field. After two circuits he calmed down and came back over to Slippers who still sat in the dust, looking very sad.

"Sorry," said Charlie, "Caught me by surprise there. Do you mean that you think you are in love with a Hedgehog?"

"Yes Charlie, I do, but how could that work? Is it allowed? What should I do next?"

Now animals don't go rushing in to a lot of fuss and nonsense straight away like the Uprights do. They take their time, until they felt they had really got an answer worth listening to. Slippers understood this.

Charlie sat quietly with Slippers, turning his long head from time to time to look at her. Slippers sat sadly beside him, wondering how she had got in to this tangle and feeling glad she had asked Charlie for advice and not Owl! The mere thought of asking Owl nearly made her squawk our loud. My goodness he would have been so cross and no help at all.

At last, Charlie said," I'm no expert on love. No experience hardly at all," he said rather sadly and pondered this for a few seconds, "But, I think, there are different sorts of love. You can *love* pulling up a juicy worm or I can *love* a crunchy carrot, we both *love* our companions here in the fields, and so I suppose I could say that a Hedgehog and a Bantam might well have a sort of Special, Loving Friendship, up to a limit you know. Do you know what I mean?"

Actually, Charlie and Slippers both had much the same outlook on *love* and all which that might include, even though neither of them had much experience. Charlie had once had a friend for a short time, name of Ed. He was very handsome indeed and had been taken off in a very smart lorry one day and rumour had it that he had gone *to Stud*. He hadn't been sure what this meant but by the nods and nudges of the stable hands and the saucy comments of some of the other horses, he had a very sketchy idea which, if it was possible, which it isn't, made him blush.

"I do know what you mean," said Slippers, "And actually I don't mind missing all that 'stuff' and having a 'Loving Friendship' instead. That sounds just perfect. Thank you so much Charlie, you've made me very happy."

"You're welcome my friend, and now, if you don't mind I think I'll have a little rest in my trailer. This sunshine is making me a bit hot and bothered you know."

10 MRS OWL GETS CROSS,

for quite a long time

After his night's hunting Owl had returned to E1693340 to share a tit-bit with Mrs Owl and have a short nap. He had found her awake and marching, which was always a bad sign.

"Good morning my love," he ventured.

"Is it?" she replied, continuing to strut about kicking up bits of poster and aiming them at a pile by the box hole.

Owl, who never learnt at which point it was wisest to remain silent said, "I think so my dear," and then rashly, "Have you had a nice rest?"

"REST!" screeched his wife, "REST, in this hovel? On this crunchy old torn up paper? My mother would turn in her grave if she knew what kind of a place I had to call home!"

On and on she went, marching and muttering, muttering and marching as the heap of paper grew higher and higher.

Owl was hurt; he had laboured long and hard pulling down the planning application posters and shredding them amongst the bedding. She had said how comfortable it was and had been most affectionate and grateful.

He sighed, "I'm sorry my dear. What about the nice soft mouse fur that you like so much?"

"How do you suppose?" . . . KICK . . . "That I can find it?" . . . KICK . . . "With all this old paper in the way! I'll have no more, do you hear? NO MORE!"

During this speech Owl had been gradually retreating backwards towards the box hole having decided to delay his nap until later.

Just as he felt the edge of the hole on his tail feathers Mrs Owl screeched, right in his face, "SO THERE!" kicking a heap of paper shreds at him.

Even in his terror he couldn't help thinking how magnificent she was when angry and, thus distracted, forgot how close he was to the hole, fell backwards and with no chance to turn round landed in a feathery heap on the barn floor.

Mrs Owl, much surprised, poked her head out of the hole, saw that he was scrambling to his feet, withdrew her head sharply and sat down in the far corner, muttering to herself but starting to feel slightly ashamed.

Once Owl had recovered his senses and got himself the right way up he shook out his feathers and glanced quickly over to the Bats, praying that they hadn't seen. He felt such a fool!

The Bats hung silently in their rows amongst the rafters, and if they had seen anything, would have pretended they hadn't, after all, it would have been very impolite to let Owl know he'd been watched.

Owl felt relieved and with one quick glance at the box, rose up and glided over to the fence.

"Thank goodness," he thought, as he landed, "A bit of peace and quiet and a sensible companion.'

Charlie ambled over, "Morning Owl"

"Morning Charlie."

Charlie looked at Owl and said, "You alright dear chap? Look a bit, well, ruffled, a bit, put about!"

Owl not realising that he was covered in dust and had bits of straw caught amongst his feathers said, "I'm fine, thank you, rather a busy night's hunting you know."

He looked down as he spoke and noticing a scrap of Planning Application stuck on one of his claws, shuffled about a bit with his back turned to Charlie until he managed to loosen it and it floated to the ground.

"Anyway," said Owl, "How did Slippers get on? Did she find a Hedgehog?"

"Oh, very well," said Charlie and he told Owl all about the meeting and the plan for Hedgehog to come over this morning to meet Charlie. Though he did not mention the blossoming love affair!

"No need for you to miss your sleep Owl. I'll see him and speak to you this evening."

"Thank you Charlie, I appreciate it. Feel a bit weary today."

The two creatures parted and, rather warily. Owl set off for E1693340 wondering what kind of reception he'd get. To his surprise and relief all was calm and orderly. Now that there were fewer paper pieces, most of them were lying on the barn floor, Mrs Owl had found the mouse fur and piled it together as a soft bed.

"Here you are my dear," she said, just as if nothing had happened, "You do look tired my love, come and rest on the bed."

"WELL!" thought Owl, "Aint females just the most aggravating of creatures and when they're expecting Owlets they're just . . . just . . . ," he could think of no suitable word and sank down on the soft furry heap, falling straight away into a warm, deep sleep.

Slippers is comforted by Sophie.

11   SLIPPERS GOES WOOING

The next morning Slipper took extra time preening and sorting her feathers and shaking out the ruffles round her feet. She had a good drink from her tray and a peck of corn and then set off to meet up with Hedgehog as arranged. It was a sparkly morning with just a touch of dew to freshen the air. She felt excited at the thought of seeing Hedgehog, and then a bit guilty as she realised that she had hardly given the Action Group, which after all was the main point of the meeting, a thought!

As she got near to the hedgerow she looked around for Hedgehog, expecting to see him nosing around in the undergrowth but there was no sign of him. She started to walk slowly along the edge of the field and suddenly saw him, rolled in to a tight ball and tucked under the overhanging leaves of an Elder bush.

"Hello!" she called and getting no reply went right over next to him and called again, "Hello, it's me, Slippers. I've come to collect you like we arranged. Charlie's looking forward to meeting you."

Hedgehog's spiny sides puffed in and out a bit faster and eventually a very small, muffled voice said, " Hello Slippers. I'm sorry to be rolled up but I can't come today. I'm too shy to come with you today!"

Well! "Too shy!" exclaimed Slippers, "Too shy? Whatever do you mean?"

"We Hedgehogs are very shy you know. I will come with you to meet Charlie but it will have to be tomorrow."

"How do you know you won't be too shy tomorrow?" Slippers was starting to sound exasperated and tried to calm down. "I mean, are you ill or something?"

"No," said the muffled voice, "Not ill, just shy which is much worse."

Now Slippers had only been ill once in her life. She remembered it well because a lot of her feathers fell out at the time. It was before she had met Mel and Darren and when they came to see her and her friends, to choose one of them to come and live with the other Hens and Charlie, she had hidden in a corner, hoping they wouldn't see how awful she looked. Mel had spotted her crouching in the dust, scooped her up and said to Darren, "This is the one for us, look, a little Bantam!" Darren had agreed that she was just right and they had driven away with her to her new home.

She still couldn't quite understand why they had picked her. Perhaps they liked bald Hens or perhaps they felt sorry for her. Either way, she didn't care because once she reached the field at Spooner Row and had room to run and scratch and friends to talk to, her feathers grew back thick and glossy and her new life had begun.

Hedgehog seemed to have all his spines so she supposed that he wasn't ill. She felt sorry for him and sorry for feeling exasperated. "Oh dear Hedgehog," she said softly, or as softly as you can when talking to a rolled up ball.

"Please don't feel shy, there's really no need."

"I know," said Hedgehog, "I will come with you tomorrow morning I promise. I won't feel shy tomorrow."

"How do you know?" said Slippers.

"Because I like you very much and I want to help the Action Group. I have promised a solemn animal promise and I will be ready tomorrow morning."

When he said he liked Slippers very much her heart gave a strange little lurch and seemed to have dropped down in to her stomach.

"That's fine Hedgehog. Don't worry any more. I will come tomorrow morning and we'll go together to see Charlie. I will look forward to it."

She did not mention Owl and the fact that he would probably screech a lot. She wouldn't see him and Charlie would smooth it over.

"See you tomorrow my dear."

Oh, how her heart did somersaults again!

"Yes," she said, "See you tomorrow, my dear Hedgehog."

Slippers fairly skipped home across the fields. How the sun shone! How the dew glistened! How wonderful her little world looked! He had called her, "My Dear".

Before she knew it, she was back home and there was Charlie looking up expectantly to greet his guest!

Charlie had already worked out that something was not quite right. Slippers looked cheery but flustered and seemed to be alone!

He hoped they hadn't had a lover's tiff already, but no she looked too happy for that.

"Hello Slippers."

"Hello Charlie," she said a bit sheepishly now that she realised she had to explain.

Charlie waited which gave Slippers time to decide how to explain but not wanting Hedgehog to be blamed or put down in any way made it a bit difficult. Oh, how she couldn't bear it if anyone was cross with Hedgehog, poor shy Hedgehog.

She took a deep breath, looked in to Charlie's soft, kindly eyes and explained.

"So you see," she was gabbling rather by the end of the tale "He will come tomorrow, he can't help being shy you know and he made a proper *animal's promise*!"

Charlie took all this in and, of course, being Charlie, understood immediately.

"I see Slippers. Hedgehogs are known for shyness and if he has promised to come tomorrow then he will come. I shall look forward to meeting him. You have done very well. Now go and get a drink and have a little rest in the shade."

Slippers could feel all her anxiety slip away.

"Thank Heaven for Charlie, my goodness how I love him," then she thought, "I must be careful what I think, a Bantam and a Hedgehog is one thing but a Bantam and a Horse is quite another!"

This made her smile, which is quite an odd look on a Bantam, and she trotted off happily with only a slight shadow of fear when she imagined Owl being told that evening! Luckily, Charlie had said he would tell Owl and make it alright with him . . . Phew!

Later that afternoon, Owl flew over to Charlie and asked how it had gone with Hedgehog.

"Did he unroll?" he asked rather rudely, it should be noted that Mrs Owl was still being rather difficult, "Does he agree? How many others can he bring in to the Group?"

Charlie, taking care to be casual and calm, finished chewing a mouthful of grass and then told Owl that Hedgehog had been too shy to come today but would come tomorrow.

"SHY!, SHY! Of all the cheek. Slippers goes all the way over there and he sits there ROLLED UP and says he's too shy! I'd give him shy, where is he, I'll go and roll him over here and see if that wakes him up a bit!" He clacked his beak, did a couple of experimental screeches and then one very loud one.

Slippers, safe in the Hen House, flinched and thanked goodness she didn't have to go out. She snuggled further in to the straw and put her wings over her ears.

After quite a bit more screeching and clacking on Owl's part and a bit more chewing and reasoning on Charlie's, things quietened down. Owl flew off to start his night's hunting and Charlie chewed on a few more tufts of grass before lying on his side and having a jolly good roll.

12   OWL'S IDEA

It was unfortunate for Slippers and Charlie that Mrs Owl was still being cross. This was upsetting Owl's sleep and generally making E1693340 rather an unpleasant place to be. Owl loved his home and his wife and hated anything that upset his happy life there.

Trouble was, he didn't know what to do and if he had known, it would still be wrong, he knew this from past experience when Mrs Owl was expecting.

Really, it was all too much. Now that he couldn't shred the posters for bedding he needed to do something else with them. He couldn't just tear them up and leave the pieces lying around on his beautiful fields and hedgerows, though Heaven knows, the Uprights did that all the time. He couldn't just leave each new poster pinned up by their field and the barn and yet, what to do? What to do?

As he flew over The Boars Pub he suddenly had an idea. Lots of Uprights went there. Quite a few of them were taken by their dogs and when they came out he had noticed that some of them were rather unsteady on their feet which made more work for the poor animals. Why did they take the Uprights at all? He would never understand this strange need that the dogs had for their Uprights. Such loyalty, such a responsibility!

Owl figured that he could pull the posters down more carefully, so they weren't too torn, fly with the poster in his beak and stick it over the odd nail or sharp twig by the pub or the Village Hall or even the Church. He flew back to the telegraph pole and sure enough, there was a fresh poster just ripe for the taking. He hovered near it and managed to perch on a bit of Hedge that had grown over towards the pole. It was hanging on by a long tendril of ivy, and by balancing precariously as if on a tight rope, he managed to carefully pull the poster off its nail.

He swooped back to the pub and looked around below him. No-one in sight. He had spotted a few old nails here and there on his night time flights and now he flew down to one not far from the door and pushed it over the nail. Not very secure but good enough for now.

Very pleased with his work he flew up and perched on top of the sheds to one side and admired the poster. A bit squint but it would puzzle the Uprights and maybe help their cause. Suddenly he saw the Hairy Upright and Robbie appear on their late night walk.

They were just passing when the Hairy Upright stopped, looked at the poster and said, "Hello Robbie, is the pub planning to extend or something? Let's have a look."

They both went over to the nail and Owl thought "Oh no, I've gone to all that trouble and now he'll pull it down."

But wait! The Hairy Upright was laughing and saying something to Robbie, "Well Robbie, look at that, how funny, how did it come to be there. That'll cause a bit of confusion. Hang on."

He rootled about in his pocket and brought out a sharp pin which glinted in the fairy lights of the pub. He reached up, straightened the poster and pushed the pin in securely. He looked down and Robbie looked up and as they walked off they both said, "Hm," under their breath in a questioning sort of way.

"Why," thought Owl, "You'd think they understood. I'm not surprised if Robbie does, I'll have a word with him about it but fancy an Upright being able to understand anything as complicated as this! I suppose some of them are brighter than others."

The next morning Slippers was up and raring to go while the dew was still wet and sparkling on the grass. She felt perfectly confident that Hedgehog would come with her today. He had made an animal promise which was not given lightly. Sure enough, as she approached the hedgerow with the Elder bushes, she spotted Hedgehog nosing around in the long grass and looking up, in a rather shortsighted way she thought, to see if Slippers was coming.

She started to walk faster, which was not easy with feathery feet, and called out to Hedgehog, "Good Morning! How nice to see you up and about."

"Good morning to you," called Hedgehog and they greeted each other affectionately. It is not easy to be affectionate if you are a hedgehog and a bantam but they managed to sort of rub nose and beak together and this felt just right.

They chatted easily as they walked slowly over to Charlie's field. Slippers reassured Hedgehog that Charlie had understood all about *shyness* and was looking forward to their meeting. Wisely, she didn't mention Owl.

Charlie had been keeping an eye out and soon spotted the little pair approaching. It made him smile to think of their love for one another but he could see that in some funny way they were well matched.

They all had a good discussion about the Animals' Action Group and what was involved. Hedgehog felt sure that some of his friends would be very willing to join in, and Charlie explained that Robin would act as messenger if Slippers couldn't get there fast enough.

Charlie was a little anxious that Hedgehog, if rolled up, wouldn't hear Robin but was reassured by him that he was very used to Robin's cheery call and could hear him perfectly well whether rolled up or not. "Quite piercing." was how he described Robin's voice and winced a little as he said it.

Slippers accompanied Hedgehog back to the hedgerow, lingered awhile and then strolled back to the field. She felt mellow and satisfied and as if life had a bit more in it these days. Funny that something so upsetting as the Planning Application seemed to have brightened all their lives.

Charlie reported back to Owl later that evening and Owl was finally well pleased. Charlie suggested that if Owl saw Slippers one morning perhaps he might thank her for her good work and Owl did just that a few days later before he went back to E1693340.

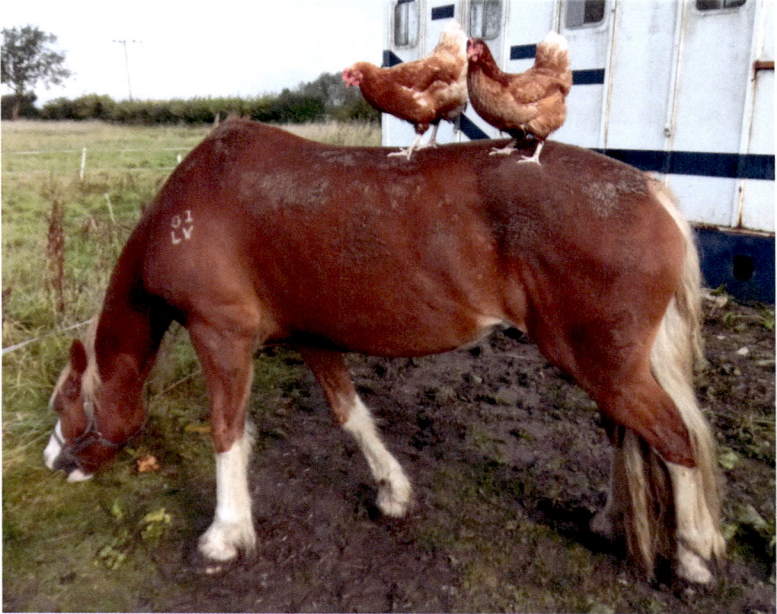

Preparing for a meeting of the Action Group.

13   ACTION BEGINS

And so now the Animals' Action Group was complete. Newts, Bats and Hedgehogs. It had taken a lot of work but they had succeeded. Of course, succeeding with the Action Group didn't mean they had succeeded with stopping the possible building work and really, the hardest part of the whole plan loomed ahead of them.

As the days passed their little patch of land gradually transformed from the quiet and rather solitary place it had been for so long. Very gradually, so that they hardly noticed the change, creatures would appear, just to pass the time of day or see if there was any news about the Day of Action as they called it. Bats would swoop over and pipe a squeaky greeting on the way to the barn. Charlie would suddenly realise that he had nearly stepped on a prickly Hedgehog or worse still a Newt. He didn't mind because it gave him someone to chat to, although he thought, "I'll never master Newt speak!"

Their peaceful world was somehow livelier, more interesting. You never quite knew what the day would bring.

One afternoon Charlie and the Hens were surprised to hear Robbie barking. Now Robbie was not one of those silly noisy dogs that fussed and yelped at every passing fly. He only barked if he wanted to communicate with Charlie and the others. Looking up they saw that the Hairy Upright had walked along the lane with another Upright they hadn't seen before.

They had stopped and leant on the top bar of the field gate and the Hairy Upright was bending down to pat Robbie's head, saying, "There, there old chap, it's ok, no need to make all that row," he turned to his friend and said, "He's quite easily startled though he knows Charlie and company well enough don't know what all the fuss is about."

Robbie did the doggy equivalent of rolling his eyes and strolled off from the two Uprights to a gap in the hedge where he could quietly talk to Charlie.

"Go over and listen to what they're saying." he said quietly, indicating the two Uprights with his nose.

Charlie and the Hens did as he said and wandered over to graze and peck around near the gate.

"Look at that," said the friend, "You'd think they had come to join in our chat!"

The Hairy Upright laughed and Robbie, job done, wandered back and sat beside him in an obedient, dog like and reassuring manner.

"Anyhow," the friend was saying to Hairy Upright, "He's a good bloke and we'd like him to come over and check a few things out for us. He'll pack up the old theodolite and get here on Thursday all being well."

The Hairy Upright said, "Well, it's a long time since I had anything to do with theodolites, they're a bit different now, laser beams and so on."

He laughed and nodded to his friend, they muttered a bit more and talked about the weather and the crops and so on and then Robbie took them off up the lane and round the corner by the rubble heap until they were out of sight.

Charlie and the Hens watched them go and then turned to look questioningly at each other. "What's a *Theobolite*?" asked Slippers.

"Theodolite," corrected Black Hen, "I don't know. Do you know Charlie?"

Charlie thought for a moment and then said, "I'm trying to remember my school days. I seem to remember one of those mentioned by a very old cart horse who used to teach us about History of the Land and all that rather boring stuff but I can't properly recall."

They all thought a bit longer and then Charlie said, "I'll ask Owl this evening. Whatever it is Owl might know and we have to be prepared."

The others nodded and shuffled off saying, "Yes, of course, Owl will know," and "They don't call them wise old owls for nothing do they!" So gradually they comforted themselves and went back to scratching and clucking and laying the odd egg.

"Hm," said Owl that evening, "Let me see. History eh? The Land mm." He paced sideways to-and-fro on the fence and looked into the distance for inspiration. "Sounds to me like those things that roamed about millions of years ago. Do you remember Charlie? Dinosaurs I think they were called."

"But," said Charlie, "If a Theodolite was one of those it couldn't have lived for millions of years could it?"

"Well, no," said Owl, "But they can pass on down all the generations you know. They might not be the same as they were then but there are beetles and bugs and so forth that go right back to those days so why not a Theodolite?" He looked triumphantly at Charlie and waited for his reply.

Charlie chewed maddeningly on a small clump of grass for a minute and then, after swallowing, said, " Goodness Owl! Do you think it would still be as big as those Dinosaurs were? We can't possibly get one of those on board with the Action Group. I mean those chaps were huge and fierce and as big as your Barn. I think. Hedgehogs and Newts are one thing but Theodolites! Phew!"

He shook his mane, snorted down his nostrils and went for a short canter round the field before continuing the conversation.

Owl, who was well used to Charlie, gave him a chance to settle down and then said, "I know what you mean old boy, but surely it can't be quite as big as all that. I think that things tend to get smaller as the years go by, and after all the Upright's friend can hardly be planning to bring something as big as the Barn over now can he! We must bite the bullet and explain to the others. We've just about got time to let the Action Group know so they can get over here and look endangered!"

"You're right," said Charlie, "We can't give up now. Robin hasn't looked in today but I'll catch him in the morning and get him to go round the Group and I'll get Hen to talk to the Newts." Then he added, "I'll ask Slippers to go over to Hedgehog as well."

Even at this frightening turn of events he hadn't forgotten that she would welcome a chance to see Hedgehog again.

"I'll tell the Bats in the morning when I get back," said Owl and rose up into the air, flying smoothly and silently off over the

Church and the village pub, then swooping swiftly down over the silent fields beyond.

Charlie didn't disturb the Hens that evening. He needed time to mull this over. He hoped there would be no violence. He hated violence, and being a peace-loving animal couldn't understand it in others. He could tell from the odd newspaper that fluttered in to the field or got left behind by someone that Uprights were very fond of violence, in fact, if the papers were right, they did little else most of the time!

He couldn't imagine the Hairy Upright fighting and in any case Robbie wouldn't let him.

"Perhaps," he mused, "the more intelligent ones don't go in for it."

He clopped up into the trailer and lay down rather wearily in the straw. He slept soundly but dreamt of great monstrous Theodolites gallumphing over the field and roaring at the little band of comrades.

14   HEN HAS A PLAN

For some days Hen had been wondering if there was anything that she could do as a sort of contribution to the Action Group. She knew that she was very helpful with the Newts and was glad of it but, was there something else she could do before the big day?

One afternoon, while strutting about the field and the hedgerows she spotted such a strange flower nodding in the breeze and the sunshine. It had a bulbous yellow bit that looked rather like a shoe for a very small Upright, but then it had long wavy dark petals hanging down each side. She went over and examined it. "No!" she thought, "No, I've never seen that before and I know all the flowers in this field. I wonder if it is *in danger*?"

She pecked around and found one or two more but that was all. "Hm, wonder if I could dig up one of these and take them back to the Hen House. I'd need to dig a hole and keep it wet. We all need to have water after all."

Hen set off back to the Hen House and after sitting and thinking for a while, she went over to the corner by the Hawthorn and nettle patch where the water feeders were set out. She took a few sips and then started to scratch at the ground by the nettles, it was quite soft because it often got water spilt on to it when Mel or one of the others topped up the feeder. She gradually scratched a nice hole and then covered it over with a few leaves and twigs. Tomorrow she would go and collect the Lady's Slipper Orchid, though of course she didn't know that was it's name and if she was very careful she would plant it in this hole and see if it would live.

All this planning and digging had made her quite tired so she took another few sips of water, pecked at a patch of corn lying nearby and then went in to the Hen House for a rest.

The next day Hen set off for the nettle patch and sure enough there was the funny looking flower nodding away at her.

She had been a little anxious in the night, "Suppose something trod on it or some daft Upright went and picked it!"

They did that she knew, they picked flowers and then as soon as they wilted or the Upright got fed up with carrying them they just chucked them on to the ground to die. It made her feel sad.

Anyhow, there it was. She was only going to take this one to see if she could keep it alive and look after it properly. She felt sure that if she could manage this, it would be another thing that the Uprights would get worked up about. It seemed to be 'in danger' and it really was very strange to look at. She poked and scraped for a long time and at last managed to get the flower out of the ground intact and with a nice fat clump of earth around it's roots. All she had to do then was to get it back safely and plant it. This proved to be quite a challenge. If she held it too hard in her beak she would break it. In the end Hen lay the little flower on the patch of nettles and by sidling up to it with one wing out managed to sort of hook it under the wing and hold it in place.

She made a strange little figure walking slowly back to the plot with one wing clamped firmly to her side and the head of the flower nestling on her feathers but she got there and dropped it thankfully in to the hole. Quickly Hen scrabbled at the heaped up earth until she had filled the hole. She patted at the ground with her foot all round the flower and then went over to the water bowl.

Now this was not easy. However hard she tried to move the bowl the weight of the feeder, which sat in it, made it too heavy for her to move. She pulled and pushed and struggled and strained and then sat down to catch her breath.

"What you doing?"

"Eh? Oh nothing."

"Don't be daft," this was Slippers, "I can see you're up to something. Where did that funny flower come from?"

Hen sighed, "Can't keep anything to yourself round here," she thought.

"Well, as it happens, I've planted this flower 'cos I thought it might be *in danger* and we could see if it would grow so the Uprights could get excited about it but it needs water and the bowl is too far away." Phew, all this explaining was far more tiring than digging up the flower!

"Oh." said Slippers, "What a good idea. Well done Hen, I'd never have thought of that."

Hen was staggered. No one usually complimented her at all and now Slippers of all Hens!

"Here, let me help." With that, Slippers grabbed hold of the dish and waited for Hen to get the other side. Between them they twisted and pulled until it moved over nearer and then they flipped their wings in the water until the earth all round the flower was good and wet, and so were the Hens.

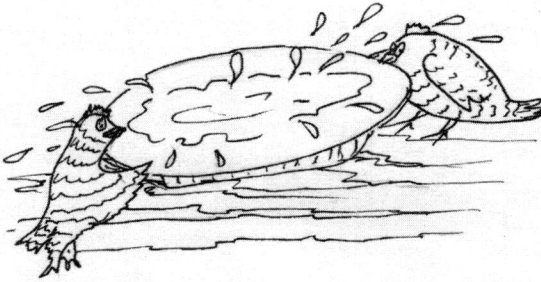

"Thanks Slippers," said Hen.

"No problem," said Slippers, flapping her wings and shaking the feathers to dry them.

"I'll help you if you let me know when it needs water."

"Tell you what," said Hen, "Let's not tell the others until we see if it lives."

Slippers agreed and Hen found that it made the whole plan more fun now that she wasn't the only one. Fancy her and Slippers being a team! How things were changing around here!

15   THE DAY OF THE THEODOLITE!

Thursday dawned bright and clear with the promise of sunshine and this suited the Animals perfectly. Between Robin, Owl, Slippers and Hen the Action Group had been alerted and were due quite soon so they could talk to Owl and Charlie and 'practise' being endangered.

Owl had cut his night's hunting short so that he could snatch a rest in E1693340 before joining Charlie and the others. The Newts were the first to arrive, probably because their legs were so short they had to allow plenty of time for the journey from the pond. There was quite a crowd of them and so long as they stuck together in fairly large groups they would be seen, hopefully! Each group was allocated two Great Crested Newts and a couple of Palmate Newts, though Charlie still couldn't see much point in the Palmates, unless they could be persuaded to lie on their backs waving their legs in the air which was hardly dignified.

Hen was rather shy about telling the others that she had planted the strange little flower and that Slippers was helping to tend it. They were all so busy marshalling the troops, getting in each other's way and generally becoming over-excited. 'They wouldn't want to hear my funny little effort." she thought modestly but then, in a quiet moment she spotted Charlie over by the fence grazing, 'keeping his strength up' he called it. Taking a deep breath she crept over to him and told him, in a rather shaky voice what she had done.

Charlie had listened carefully, with his long head lowered the better to hear her.

When she finished her tale with, "So you see Charlie, I know it's not much but Slippers agreed it might help. What do you think?"

Her beady little eyes turned up to his great head and he said, "Hen, what wonderful idea! How clever of you to think of it and how good of Slippers to help. It's the final detail! Well done indeed!" You can imagine how pleased Hen felt at this praise.

"But Charlie," she said, "It's so delicate. Suppose someone treads on it?" She was thinking partly of Charlie but didn't want to say it.

"I shall keep a special eye out for your little flower. I'll trot over in a sec. And have a look at it. Don't worry, I'll head anyone off who gets too near, but we must try to make sure they see it." With that he trotted over to the water feeder and peered at the Slipper Orchid from his great height.

Meantime, the Bats had done a couple of practise swoops low over the field and even thrown in a couple of barrel rolls like an air display team. They had retreated back to the Barn to wait the signal Owl would give, two loud screeches. They were quite excited by the whole thing and the novelty of going out in daylight added to it.

They jostled back on the rafters, calling out to each other, "How about doing an extra Barrel roll?"

"No, how about throwing in a figure of eight over the Hen House?"

At last, an older Bat said, "Settle down now. We're supposed to look natural you know. Mustn't make the Uprights suspicious. You know what they're like, they worry a lot and start arguing and shouting. Best to keep them calm. Mind you," he added with a grin, "Won't hurt to have a bit of fun will it!"

The others laughed and after a bit more jostling and adjusting of wings they settled quietly in the dusty gloom to listen for Owl's signal.

The Hedgehogs were well represented and Slippers with her head held very high, was at the front of their troupe with Hedgehog. Once they had arrived and greeted everyone they rolled up in to balls dotted around the enclosure like so many footballs.

Owl eyed them disapprovingly, "What's the point of coming and then rolling up in to balls?"

"No matter," said Charlie, "They explained that they can hear perfectly well and as soon as Owl screeches they'll unroll and start nosing around. It'll be fine, don't worry."

"Mmm," said Owl and clacked his beak a couple of times.

"No screeches!" Charlie shouted quite loudly, "Not yet, you'll set the whole lot off too soon."

Owl closed his beak and pulled his face into the ruff of feathers at his neck.

Charlie said to him, "Owl, when we see the lorry or van coming we'll have an idea of the size of the Theodolite won't we?"

"Yes," said Owl quietly, "Glad that Charlie was talking to him again, "I wish we knew more about this creature. I couldn't really find out much at all. I asked other Owls and a few foxes, they're pretty sharp fellows. I even asked the odd rabbit but they really are quite dim you know."

Charlie nodded gravely, he knew!

The sun rose and began to warm the field and the trailer. Charlie had gone back in for a quiet think but as the trailer warmed up and the straw glowed a soft golden yellow he found his head starting to nod. Falling asleep on the job would never do. He was on duty today, on high alert and shaking his head and snorting he trotted down the ramp and round his enclosure a couple of times, not an easy thing to do when you had to avoid Newts and rolled up Hedgehogs. And so he settled down for a quiet graze, casting the odd glance over to the lane when he heard an engine.

Just as they had all began to get a bit bored and worried a loud, rattly engine could be heard and something made them all (except the Hedgehogs) look up expectantly. Quite a small scruffy van drew up and pulled in by the five-bar-gate. An Upright got out, stretched and looked up at the sun. Owl watched carefully, should he screech now? It felt too soon. He would wait until the Theodolite and the Upright were in the field.

The Upright opened the back door of the van and pulled out a bundle of quite long sticks and a large black bag that seemed quite heavy. He unlocked the padlock on the gate and, with a bit of trouble managed to get himself, the heavy box and the bundle of sticks through the gate before it swung to. The sticks were a bright, almost luminous yellow!

Where was the Theodolite? Was it still in the van? What was in the big black bag? They waited.

The Upright turned his back on Charlie, knelt down and started tutting and rummaging about in the bag. He stood up and carried on assembling something that they couldn't see too clearly.

Just as he finished, they heard the Hairy Upright calling out. "Hello Fred, heard you were coming over. Thought me and Robbie would see how you were getting on!"

The Uprights greeted each other in a friendly manner and the Upright who had finished assembling things by now, strolled over to the gate for a chat.

Goodness! Charlie and Owl were transfixed. Owl had been getting ready to screech but shut his beak with a snap and looked at Charlie. The Yellow sticks now supported a creature with a large bright orange head covered in knobs and screws and a huge protruding central eye!

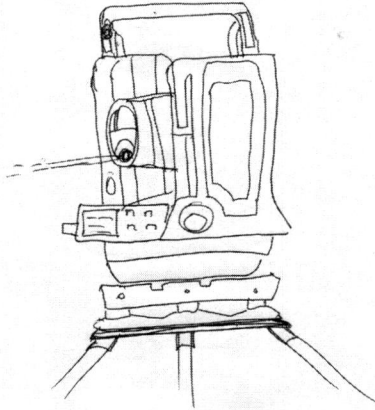

Robbie had moved quietly away from the Hairy Upright and was peering through a gap in the hedge, just as flummoxed as the others.

Charlie said to Owl, "This creature reminds me of a Parrot I once saw years ago. It had escaped from an Upright and it was all sorts of colours, yellows and greens and reds. Someone said it was Tropical, from somewhere far away. Do you think this Theodolite is Tropical and why does it need so much help? The Upright is like its keeper. It seems very docile. What do you think Owl? What should we do?"

"Wait a sec," said Owl, "At least it doesn't seem fierce. Hang on, look, its keeper has stopped talking. He's going over to it."

They watched, Owl was bursting to let off his two loud screeches but he and Charlie seemed rooted to the spot.

The Keeper had picked up the Theodolite which clearly was unable to walk unaided on it's three legs, and set it down gently in a different spot. Was it ill they wondered. The Keeper now started fiddling with its eye! Good grief, what on earth was he doing, couldn't it even see without assistance?

The Keeper stood behind it, bent over and peering and quite suddenly a red beam burst forth from its eye and went in the direction of the trailer! Charlie bridled and snorted, Owl let out two enormous screeches and all hell broke loose.

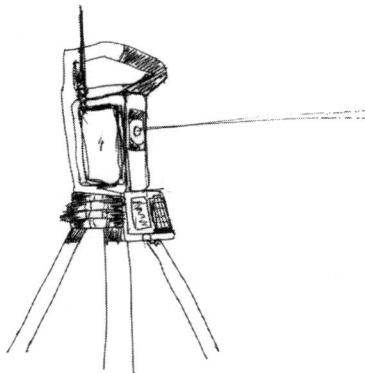

The Bats streamed menacingly out of the Barn, squeaking and swooping low over the Keeper and The Tropical Theodolite. The Hedgehogs unrolled instantly and began marching prominently around the enclosure, occasionally rolling up in unison and then unrolling on cue, to form a procession. The Newts in their anxiety to be seen were forming a sort of motorcycle display team by piling up on top of each other with the Great Crested Newts on the top and the Palmates waving their feet.

The Horseshoe bats had detached from the main swarm and were performing a sort of double act, alarmingly near to the keeper who had retreated in astonishment but not before the Tropical Theodolite had shot out another death ray from it's fearsome orange head.

The Hairy Upright and Robbie were transfixed. What a show! They had never seen anything like it.

Charlie, stood taking all this in. He looked over at the Death Ray Tropical Theodolite. He felt scared but angry, a most unusual feeling for Charlie. He hardly recognised 'angry' but he quite liked it. It made him feel reckless, it made him feel brave. A wonderful idea had entered his head and, while the Keeper retreated further over so that he could talk to Hairy Upright ,Charlie started sidling quietly over towards the alien creature. He felt that at any moment it might turn that terrible eye in his direction and shoot out a death ray at him but somehow, he didn't care. He must act quickly before they were all killed. Black Hen and Slippers, who had been jumping up and down until the first death ray, were now clucking fiercely from the underneath his trailer but as they saw him sidling over towards the monster they fell silent. Hen was over by the water feeder pacing nervously from side to side like a goalkeeper, protecting her flower.

The Hairy Upright took in the extraordinary scene and saw Charlie starting to sidle over. The Keeper said to him, "I've never seen such a collection of creatures all in the same spot! Is it always like this?"

Hairy Upright put an arm on the Keeper's shoulder and said, "Well, I suppose it's a bit busier today than usual but this area does have an amazing collection of species you know. Not just the Animals but the Flora."

"Eh?" said the Theodolite Keeper who didn't know much about wild flowers.

"Over there," said The Hairy Upright who had spotted the little flower in the corner near Robbie, "That," he said dramatically,

"If I'm not mistaken is a rare species of orchid called Lady's Slipper."

The Keeper tried to look impressed but couldn't take much more in.

 The Hairy Upright pointed an arm dramatically in the direction of the field on the other side of the lane,

"Much the same over there you know. Lots of 'em, growing wild!" This wasn't actually true but sounded good so he thought he'd throw it in, "Can you see up above the stand of trees, I think that's quite a rare Hawk isn't it?"

The Keeper followed the pointing arm and squinted into the far distance. For all he knew it might be a Golden Eagle! Nothing would surprise him today.

Charlie saw that the Hairy Upright was distracting the Keeper and Robbie was keeping an eye on the Action Group and an eye on his Upright, so he continued to sidle up the enemy. Suddenly, he turned his back on the Theodolite and with all his force, which was considerable, kicked out with his back legs at the skinny yellow legs of the creature.

CRACK!! The Keeper and the Hairy Upright turned back to the field, the Action Group stood absolutely rooted to the spot, even the Bats seemed to hover in a black cloud over their heads.

The Tropical Theodolite trembled and then folded at the knees and fell to the ground and it's big orange head fell off!

Every creature in the field yelled, "Hooray! Hooray!" or the animal equivalent. Charlie snorted and neighed, the Hens cackled and crowed. The Newts and Hedgehogs snorted and squished, though you couldn't really hear them. Robbie barked and howled. The Bats squeaked and clacked their leathery wings together, performing aerial acrobatics in the sky and over it all, Owl and Mrs Owl who had come out to join him, screeched and screeched and screeched in triumph.

The Keeper had bundled the poor, pathetic injured Tropical Theodolite back in to his van, slammed the back doors shut and rattled off up the lane as fast as he could go, which, as the van was very old wasn't very fast.

The Hairy Upright was leaning on the top of the gate, nodding to himself and smiling as if to say, "Well done, my friends, well done."

Robbie trotted over to him and looked up as if to say, "Thank you." Then he and the Hairy Upright turned their heads for home.

Charlie wonders where the Action Group should go from here!

16 WHAT'S NEXT?

Owl and Charlie found that as the days passed they began to feel a bit uneasy. The Day of the Theodolite had been a great success, but what now? Surely that wouldn't be the end of it. Each time Owl moved the poster to a different location another would appear on the telegraph pole so the Council Uprights hadn't given up. They had a chat about it one morning as Owl was headed to E1693340.

"Been thinking," said Owl

"Mmm, me too," said Charlie.

"What should we do now?" they both said together.

"Thing is Owl, it's all very well injuring the Theodolite and putting on a good show but we don't know how the Uprights work. What is their next step?"

"Well Charlie, how about we have a word with Robbie next time he takes the Hairy Upright for a walk. The Theodolite Keeper and the Hairy Upright seemed to know each other. Perhaps they talk and if they did I'm sure Robbie would listen in. We have to be ready for anything."

"Good idea Owl, Robbie brings him this way most days. Haven't seen them yet but I'll keep watch. By the way, " Charlie shuffled about rather awkwardly and examined his hooves, "I've felt a bit bad, a bit worried. I didn't mind wounding the Theodolite but, do you think I've killed him?"

" No, no Charlie, not with that great big hard head?"

"But it fell off," said Charlie, pawing at the ground and snorting.

"So what, that Keeper bloke fixed it on in the first place, it was in a bag wasn't it?"

"True, true," said Charlie, "I'd forgotten that."

"Well then, there's an end to it. It'll be right as rain and probably off somewhere else by now, frightening some other creatures to death. Pity you didn't kill it if you ask me. Anyhow," he yawned, "I'm off to my bed."

Owl was a little wary nowadays when returning to E1693340 which was a pity because he had always thought of it as his peaceful haven, safe and snug, just him and his dear wife. Since her hysterical outburst about the torn up posters he had taken care not to upset her but this was proving a strain at times.

Today, he put one careful foot over the wooden ledge and called out softly, "Hello my dear, how are you?" To his surprise his wife was sitting calmly by a freshly plumped pile of bedding.

A little tit-bit awaited him in the other corner and she pointed to it with a claw and said, "I've put you a little snack , you must be so tired. The bed is all ready for you."

Mrs Owl looked at him fondly, which made Owl feel distinctly nervous, "Why thank you," he said as he went over to the corner, picked up the remains of a dead mouse and chewed quietly.

"I've been thinking," Mrs Owl said.

Owl promptly choked on the mouse and retreated further in to the corner.

"I've been thinking, that our bed would be so much nicer if you could go back to filling it up a bit with the torn up posters you used to bring. So lovely and soft they were."

Owl thought of all the night's hunting time he had wasted searching out odd nails and hooks to fix the posters to. He thought how sometimes he had to have several goes to get the things fixed properly and how last night a nail had poked him in the eye. He was on the verge of exploding into a volley of screeches when suddenly it occurred to him that this Mrs Owl was far easier to live with than the other version and if she wanted him to go back to bringing the posters home for the bedding then so much to the good. He could get more hunting done and all would be harmony in E1693340!

"Why of course I can do that my dear, no problem at all," he edged over to the bed and sank down on to it thankfully. He really was so very tired.

Mrs Owl went over to his side, saying, "I'm a little weary myself Owl, I think I'll join you."

So side by side, curled in a feathery heap they lay and slept.

17 FRED VISITS THE BOSS

Fred the Theodolite keeper had driven away as fast as his little van would take him on that extraordinary day. He drove straight back to Norwich to meet his boss, Arthur.

Now Arthur was a busy man, after all he ran a big building company and had done so for many years.

When Fred came in to his office he said, "Hello there, take a seat, you look rather hot and bothered."

"Hello Arthur," Fred said, "Hot and bothered, I should say I am! Never had a site visit like that before, what's more me theodolite's bust and that'll cost a pretty penny." He flopped down in to the chair.

Arthur looked at some notes on his desk, "You only went to a field at Spooner Row Fred. What do you mean 'your theodolite's bust?' What on earth have you been up to?"

Fred took a deep breath and launched in to his extraordinary tale of Newts and Bats, Hens and Hedgehogs and Horses and throwing in Mr and Mrs Owl as an afterthought.

"Do you expect me to believe that all these creatures were packed in to one small field Fred? You didn't happen to stop off at the Boars on your way there did you?"

"No I did not!" said Fred "I'm not tellin' you no lies neither."

His grammar was slipping in the heat of the moment. "I tell you it's like a sort of bloomin' nature reserve – even got a peculiar lookin' flower, I nearly trod on it but those Hens went at my ankles, peckin' and snappin' at me. Had to admire them you know," spluttered Fred.

"I think you need a bit of a break, Fred, take the Missus and get off on the Broads for a week or two."

"You don't understand," said Fred, "That place – the pond, the barn and a beautiful horse you know, sort of tan colour with big brown eyes and long legs; and those Newts! Enough to make a cat laugh. I tell you Arthur," he sat back in the chair and gazed up at the ceiling, "It felt like those creatures were defending the place or something. Never seen the like. Magical sort of place it was." He sank into silence, chuckling slightly.

Arthur looked at him in amazement. "Fred," he said gently, as if talking to an amiable but possibly dangerous lunatic, "What do you want me to do? I can't get over there myself, too busy, you know how it is, but how about I give a mate of mine, Malcolm a call? He might get over there. Works for the Council, on the Environmental Team. I certainly can't afford the money or the bad press you get once the protestors get involved and I don't want to get in to a job that's doomed from the start."

He walked round the desk starting to usher Fred towards the door.

Just as he managed to get him half way through, Fred turned back and said, "You should have seen those Hens Arthur, what a laugh – there was this little one, feathery feet you know . . . "

Arthur patted him on the shoulder, propelled him in to the corridor and banged the door shut behind him.

"Phew, never thought old Fred would start cracking up like that, he's no age, not even 60! Still," he thought picking up the phone, "Better give Malcolm a ring and see when he can get over to Spooner Row."

A couple of evenings later Arthur phoned the Hairy Upright at home. They had worked together at South Norfolk Council years ago and he remembered that his old pal lived in Spooner Row.

Robbie was drowsing on the hearthrug when the phone rang. The Hairy Upright's wife Betty answered the call and then, smiling, waved the receiver at her husband. He listened for a while, nodding occasionally and absent-mindedly patting Robbie who had sidled over to sit next to him. Luckily Arthur's voice could be heard distinctly and Robbie soon began to get the drift of the call. He edged closer and leant quite heavily against his charge's leg. The Hairy Upright looked down at him, smiled and said, "What's this you soppy old thing?" Amazing how affectionate a dog can be, he thought, quite unaware that Robbie had other motives.

"What's that Arthur? Oh right, yes that's fine, see you and Malcolm at 10 a.m. Tuesday. I'll meet you in the field."

He replaced the phone.

The following morning was bright and fresh. Robbie took the Hairy Upright for his morning walk a little earlier than usual; they were both keen to get out in to the air.

"Hold hard Robbie," called Hairy Upright, as his companion trotted briskly forward, eager to see Charlie and perhaps Owl if he was lucky.

He obligingly slowed his pace, making allowances for his Upright who, after all, was getting on in years. They soon reached the field and walked quietly up to it, they had spotted Owl on the fence with Charlie close beside him.

"Quiet now Robbie," said the Hairy Upright, "We mustn't frighten the Owl."

"Humph!" thought Robbie, "if you knew Owl you'd be the one to be frightened!"

He sidled back a few feet and poked his nose through a gap in the hedge. Charlie strolled quietly towards him, if a horse could have whistled nonchalantly he would have, but instead he settled for a casual gaze around at the sky with an occasional chew of a piece of carrot he had spotted earlier.

The Hairy Upright was still looking at Owl with such a look of wonder that Robbie thought, "It's just an Owl, why are Uprights so excited about Owls?"

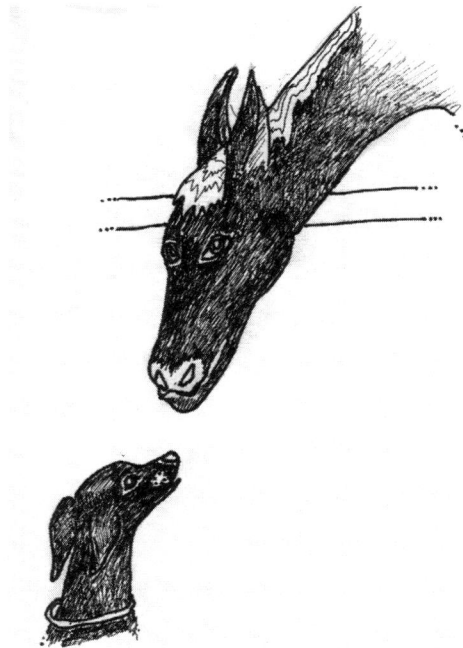

Ah, here was Charlie now, bending his neck to put his long face down to Robbie's nose. Animals, unlike Uprights, did not have to chatter and gossip generally. They thought before speaking and only used a few well-chosen words if the situation needed it.

Robbie, who had seen detective programmes on the Upright's TV and knew the drill, whispered out of the side of his mouth, darting furtive looks at Owl and the Hairy Upright.

"Tuesday morning, 10am. Important Yellow Hat coming."

Charlie looked at Robbie and doing his best to make the same shape mouth which is not easy when you are a horse, said "Are you ok Robbie? Look a bit odd this morning."

Robbie sighed, "I'm being secret, did you hear me, 10am on Tuesday morning, it's important!"

"Ah, sorry old chap," boomed Charlie. The Hairy Upright looked over at them and called for Robbie to, "Heel!"

"Ridiculous expression," thought Robbie but with a last meaningful look at Charlie he dutifully trotted up to the Hairy Upright, treating him to one of his sorrowful, apologetic looks.

"There, there Robbie, I'm not cross and the Owl has gone in to the barn now. Come along." Robbie switched to his cheerful face and wagged his tail as they headed round Top Common to find Betty waiting with a nice warm hearth rug for him and a coffee for Hairy Upright.

Charlie trotted over to the Hen House. His mind was racing. Another Yellow Hat. They'd have to get the message round the Action Group pronto! He knew Robin would appear quite soon and kept a look our for him. He would tell the Hens now. They were just beginning to emerge from the Hen House, fluttering their feathers and looking around with their sharp little eyes.

Charlie soon filled them in. They had time to get a good show together but this time it had to be a bit more 'natural looking.'

The Hens took on the task of seeing the Newts and Hedgehogs. Slipper needed no encouragement to do this and started preening her feathers and shaking off the dust straightaway.

Owl would have to be told this evening before his foraging trip and he would tell the Bats. Robin had appeared and duly flew off to rouse up any Hedgehogs or Newts who were out and about.

Hen checked on her Special Flower by the water bowl and was pleased to see a new bud and tiny fresh green leaves. She splashed a bit of water on to it and made a mental note to keep an eye on this Yellow Hat who was bound to be just as clumsy as the other one had been. Funnily enough, it wasn't so hard this time to contact the Group because several of them often dropped in during the day to catch up on progress and have a bit of a mardle.

The settled world of Charlie's field seemed to have become quite a hub of activity. By the time Tuesday morning arrived the Action Group was primed and ready. They had had a good meeting to discuss tactics and considering the variation in size and speech of all the different creatures it was quite surprising how well it went. Could it be that over recent weeks they had started to get used to each other's ways? Who would think that a Newt would call out a cheery "Good Morning!" to an Owl or a Horse would say, "Oh excuse me Old Chap!" as he stepped daintily over a rolled up Hedgehog!

At least they knew roughly what to expect this time. They had no anxieties about unknown monsters like the Theodolite, though Charlie still woke up in the night sometimes with nightmares about big orange heads flying off and rolling towards him.

18   THE ENVIRONMENTAL YELLOW HAT

When the van appeared and the Yellow Hat got out they slid in to action like a well-oiled machine. They waited until he was in the field and then they waited a bit longer while he greeted Hairy Upright and Robbie who had happened along.

Gradually one or two Hedgehogs strolled across to Charlie and nosed about by the trailer. The Yellow Hat might not have noticed but, as luck would have it, the Hairy Upright spotted them and pointed them out.

"By Jove," he said, "Haven't seen a Hedgehog out in the open for a long time. Just look at that Horse, you'd think he knew they were there!"

Robbie rolled his eyes and sighed. The Hens fluttered and clucked round the Yellow Hat until they succeeded in herding him over to the little Orchid by the water bowl, rather like 'One Dog and his Man' on the TV.

"Hey!" he called out to the Hairy Upright, "Come and look at this!"

Hairy Upright went over and joined him, dropping a trail of corn for the Hens as he walked. "Ah," he said knowledgeably, "A Lady's Slipper Orchid, very rare those."

"You don't say," said the Yellow Hat, "Fancy it growing here!

A small procession of Great Crested Newts marched across behind the flower and this time the Yellow Hat made no comment! He put his hands on his hips and gazed up at the sky just as Owl flew across closely followed by a stream of bats. The Horsehoes flew low, narrowly missing the Yellow Hat and before he could exclaim to Hairy Upright they had vanished in to the barn.

"Did you see that?" he called, "Have you ever seen Owls and Bats flying out together in the day time?"

"Oh yes," said Hairy Upright casually, "They live in the Barn. See them most days sometime or other, mostly in the evening of course," he added helpfully.

After the Yellow Hat had jumped back into his van and rattled off round the common and back to the Council Offices Robbie barked his congratulations and the Animals settled down and wandered about the field, gathering in groups, saying, "Well done Hedgehogs," and " Good on you Hens," while others blushed and looked down saying, "Oh it was nothing you know." Owl and the Bats flew in to the Barn, calling softly to each other so as not to disturb Mrs Owl who was getting near the time when she would deliver her new brood. At last sleep overtook them and peace descended.

Malcolm wasted no time getting back to Arthur the Builder and telling him all about the field and the creatures and flowers that lived there. Arthur had listened patiently, letting him blither on for a while and then put the phone down. As we know, Arthur, the Business Upright had a big building company and lots of money but he was no fool. He did not want aggravation, demonstrations and angry people poking him with placards.

So, rubbing his chin and swivelling about in his office chair, he thought, "It would do me no harm if I called up the

Environmental Team once they hear back from Malcolm and make it clear that I would not consider building on this important site because I am concerned about Endangered Flora and Fauna (Animals and Plants) and am very keen on Conservation and so on.

"Why," he thought, swinging back the other way and gazing at the ceiling, "Might even get my picture in the local paper, or even the national press! I'd be a sort of Animal Saviour, and an all round jolly good egg!

"I'd like that. I'd like that very much. Wonder if I might get an award from the Queen? Lord and Lady Arthur Phipps!"

It had quite a ring to it he thought!

19   A SITE OF SPECIAL SCIENTIFIC INTEREST!

Now, the world of Uprights, as we all know, is full of nonsense. Nothing is normally straightforward, Uprights rarely say exactly what they actually mean and often have an ulterior motive.

Instead of two or three Uprights getting together and having a talk, they usually set up committees and forums and 'hubs'! They spend a lot of money hiring very boring rooms in very boring buildings so they can discuss things and argue and disagree. They usually stop half way through for a boring buffet, which they pretend to enjoy and then they go back to arguing and writing things down on post-it-notes so they can stick them on a wall and look at them!

Of course Animals don't know much about this, though I don't think they'd be surprised. They would however think it all very wasteful and time-consuming. Why, a horse could crop the grass, chat to his comrades, gallop about and gaze at the moon as it appeared on a summer's evening in a fraction of the time the poor old Uprights have wasted, but such is life!

The upshot of the previous weeks of effort, anxiety and planning by the animals was that their little home became registered as an S.S.S.I. Uprights like initials – they sound important, and make people who don't know what they mean feel silly.

Arthur the builder had been true to his word. He had applied to the right departments and accompanied more yellow hats to the field. He had filled out forms and promised to fulfil all sorts of requirements listed endlessly on bits of paper. Owl would have had them shredded in a trice! It all rather made his head spin!

Sometimes, Arthur wondered what on earth he was doing. He didn't need all this extra work which didn't pay anything at all. When he felt really worried and uncertain he would get in his car and go to Charlie's field. He always took carrots and apples for

Charlie and corn for the Hens. He liked to go in the early evening as the day was fading. He would sit on the edge of Charlie's trailer and listen to the sound of peace, which he hadn't heard for years and years it seemed. Sometimes he would see the odd Newt or Hedgehog. Usually, if he waited for dusk Owl and a few Bats would fly over on their silent, sweeping wings. It almost made him want to cry sometimes, which of course he didn't do because tough, yellow hat, business Uprights couldn't possibly behave in such a way. He didn't know why he felt like that and decided that there was something magical in this place and left it at that.

By the time he had said goodbye to the animals and got back in his grand car he knew exactly why he was doing this strange thing and was glad.

As for Charlie and his friends, they knew little of this. Their world had changed and they no longer needed to alert the Action Group or send Robin out to round them up. Most days, quite a few of them were in the field anyway at one time or another. Hen's Orchid had not just survived but thrived and she had hopes of a colony of these pretty things in the corner by the water bowl.

The Horseshoe bats and some of the others had gone back to Devon but had promised to return for their holidays next year and those that remained in the Barn were now well bedded in, and were great pals with Mr and Mrs Owl who were very busy bringing up their brood of owlets. Mrs Owl had settled down nicely and Owl was kept busy, foraging at night to keep them all fed. Even Mrs Owl took her turn at this leaving Owl warily in charge of the nest.

The Newts still squished and fizzed around by their pond and made the long trip across the field as often as they could.

Slippers and Hedgehog remained good and loving friends and saw each other most days either alone or with other Hedgehogs who had popped over. This didn't 'cramp their style' much because they were mostly rolled up in balls anyway.

The Animals noticed that there seemed to be more Uprights than usual, leaning on the fence rail or peering through the hedgerow but welcomed their coming. There were no more planning posters for Owl to pull down and shred. The only new notice was one which explained about this 'Area of Special Scientific Interest' which made very little sense to any of them, even to Owl.

As Owl said to Charlie and the Hens, " Don't rightly know what it says but I think it means we're safe." And it did.

The seasons turned round. The long hot days of summer faded into the blackberries and rosehips of gentle autumn and then on to winter. Mel, Darren, Sophie and Luke, and their friend Tallulah, were happy that this strange thing had come to pass. And although, in their busy lives it wasn't easy to get over to see the Animals every day, they always managed to find the time because they knew that it had brought them something that they would always remember.

And it all worked out well in the end, Mel, Luke and Sophie can still enjoy the fields and Charlie and his friends are safe.

THE END